MEZZO ZENTANGLE DESIGNS

Copyright © 2021
All rights reserved. No part of this publication may be reproduced, distributed, or transmitted in any form or by any means, including photocopying, recording, or other electronic or mechanical methods, without the prior written permission of the publisher.

MEZZO
ZENTANGLE
DESIGNS

MEZZO
ZENTANGLE
DESIGNS

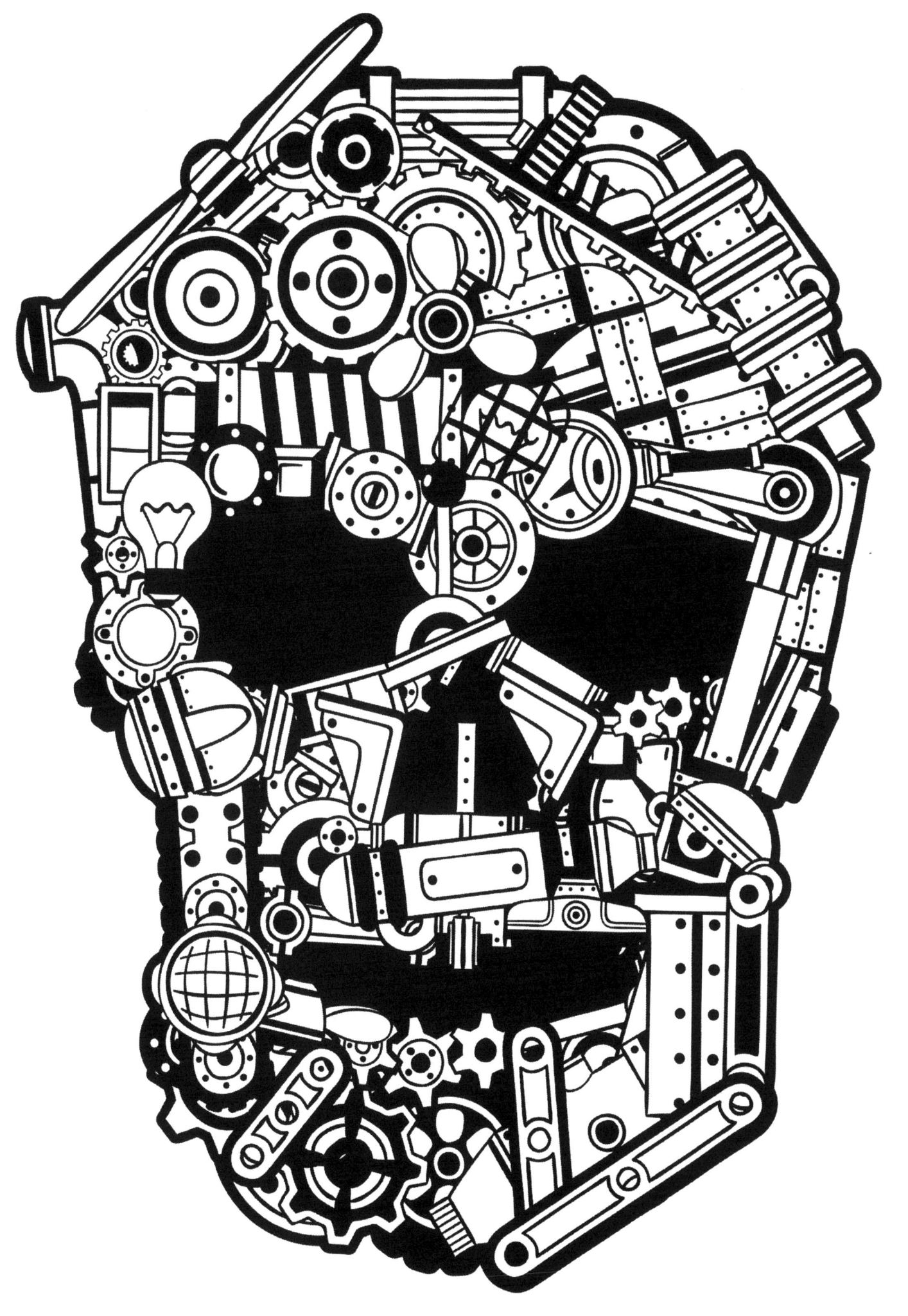

MEZZO
ZENTANGLE
DESIGNS

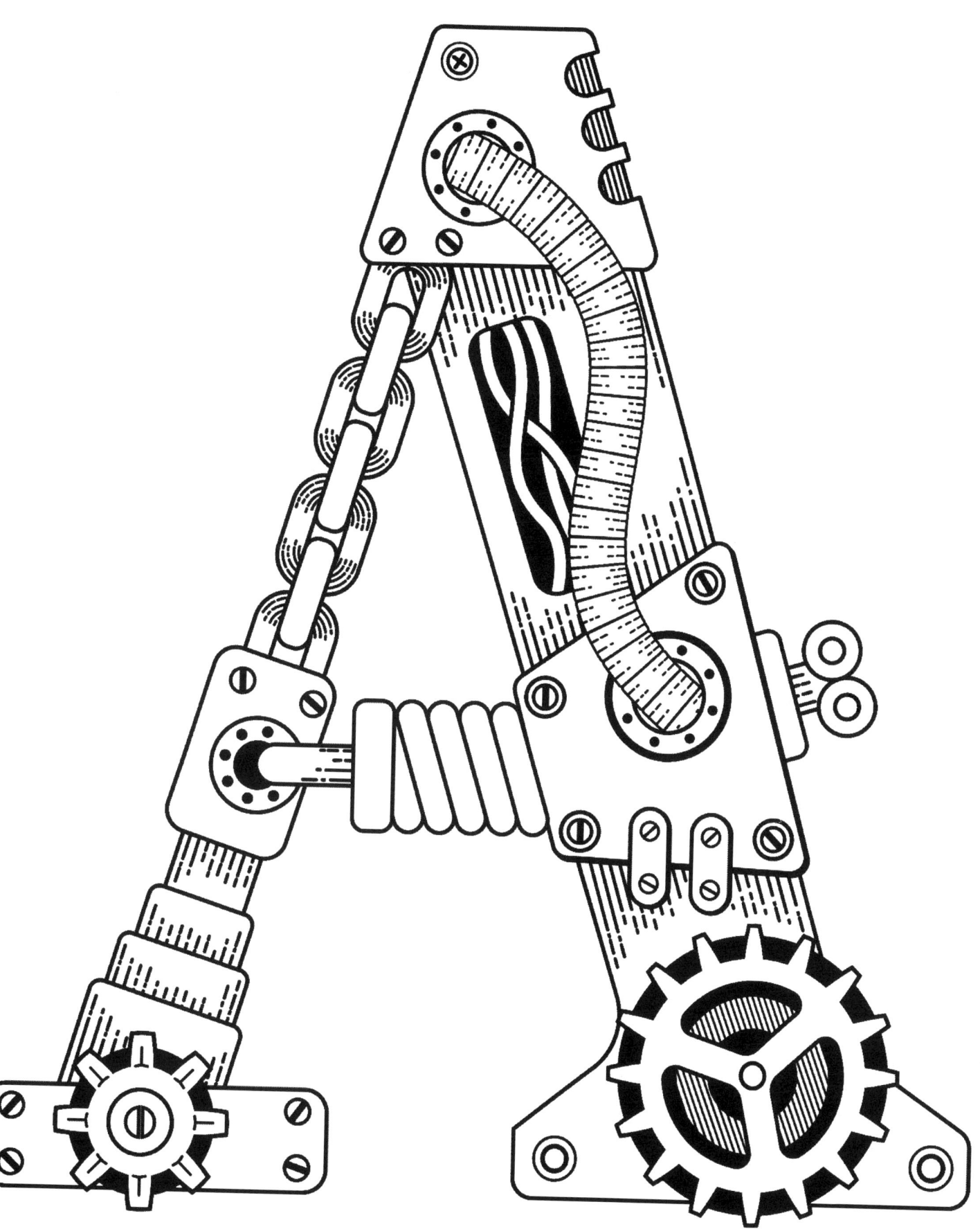

MEZZO
ZENTANGLE
DESIGNS

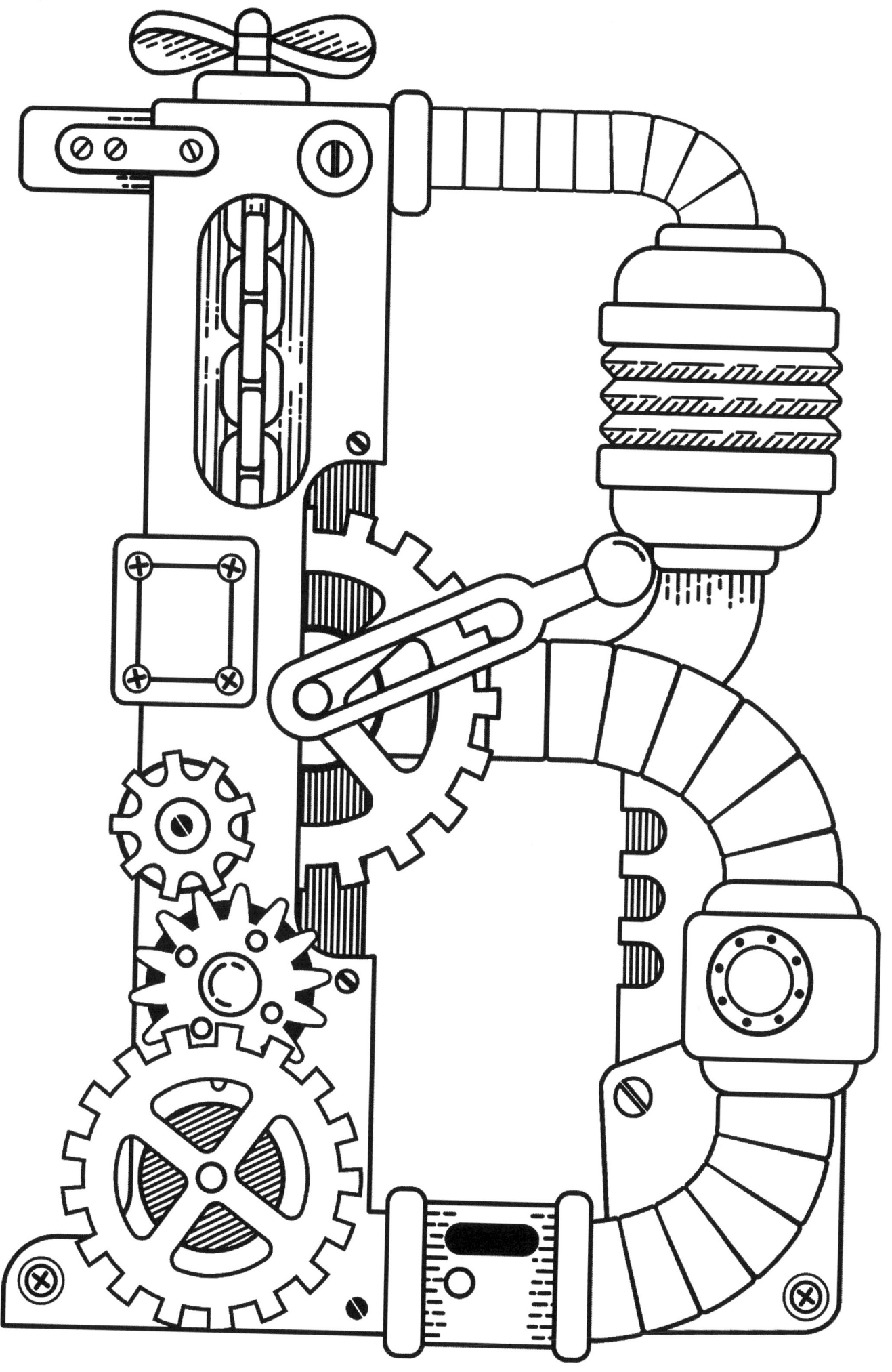

MEZZO
ZENTANGLE
DESIGNS

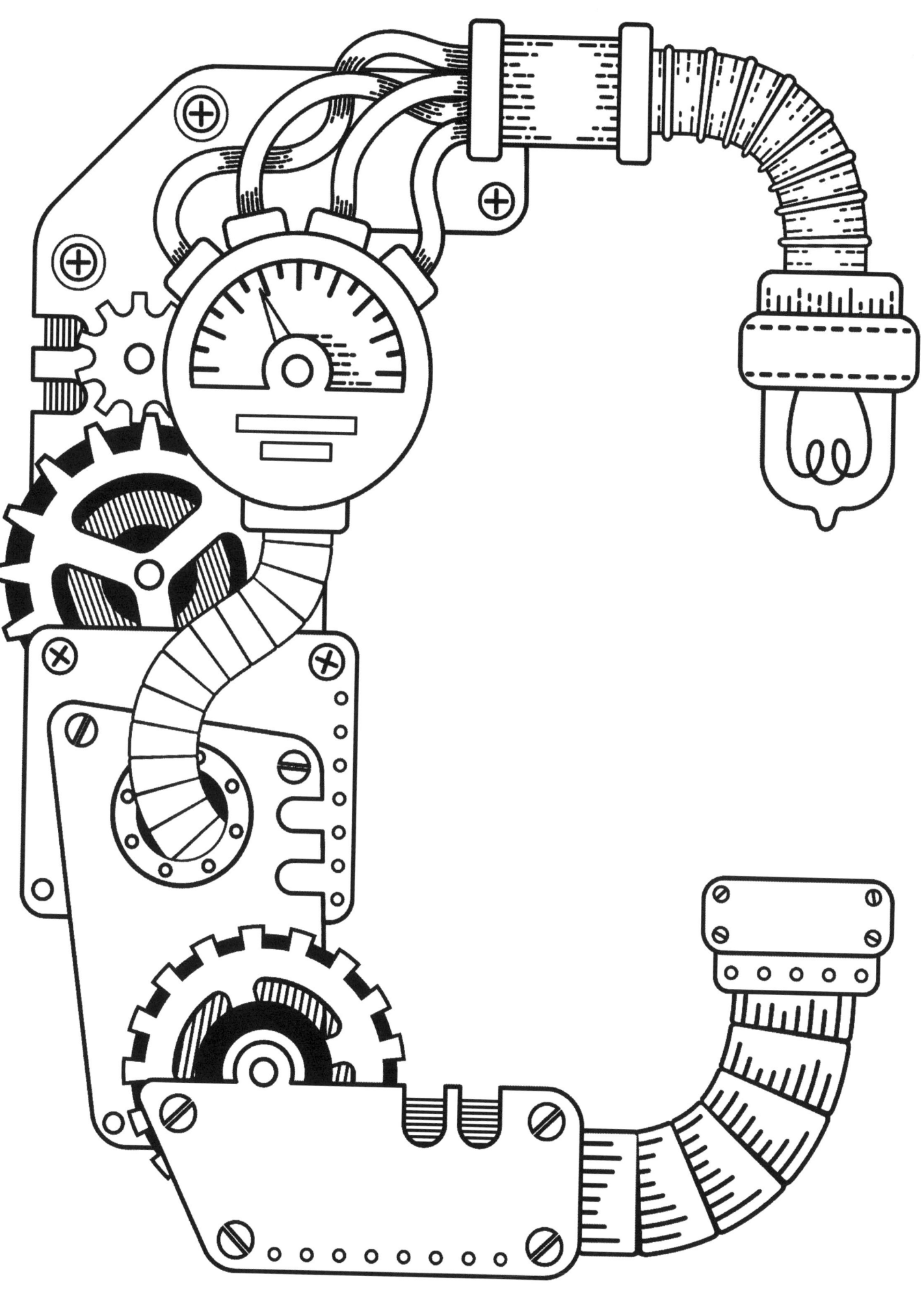

MEZZO
ZENTANGLE
DESIGNS

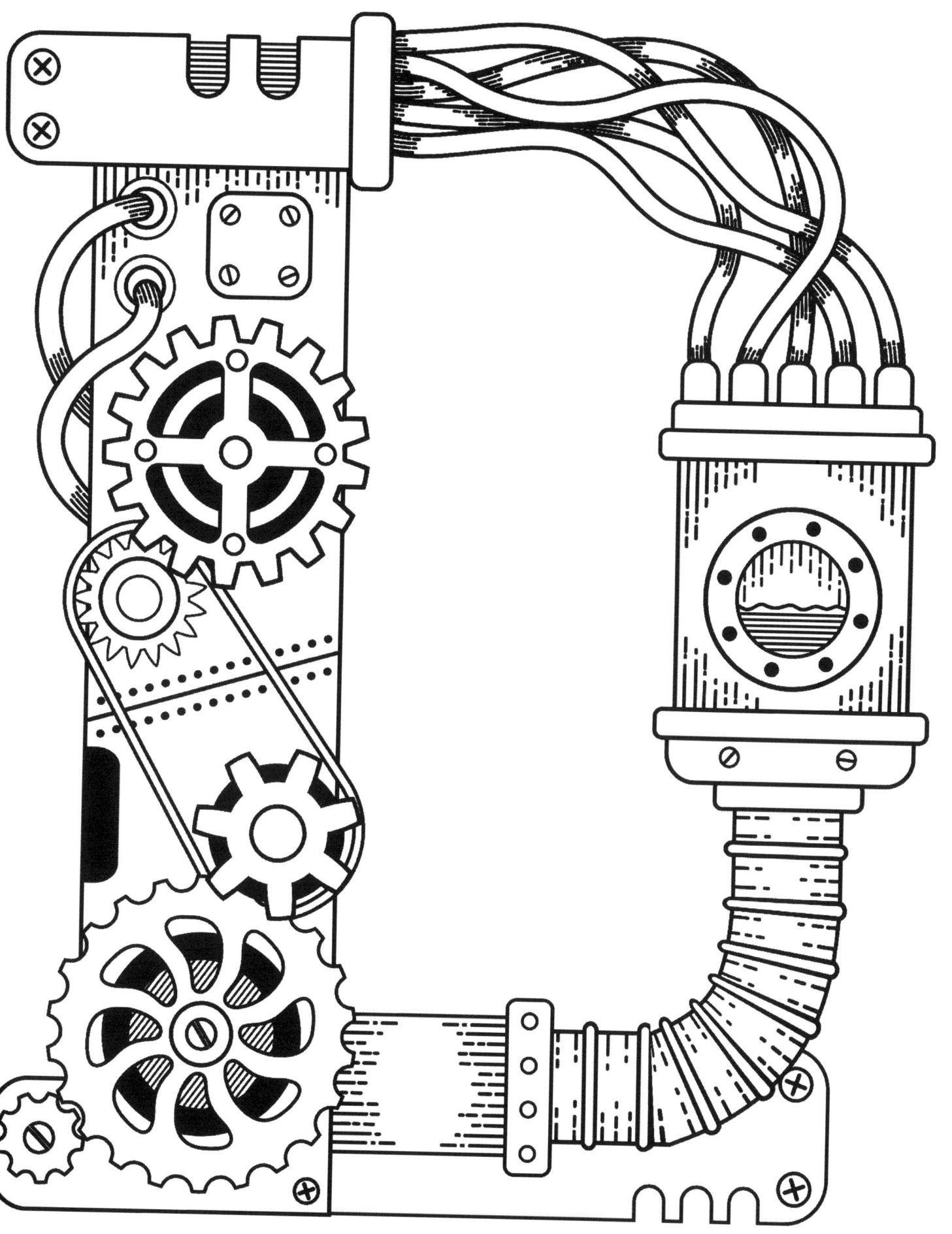

MEZZO
ZENTANGLE
DESIGNS

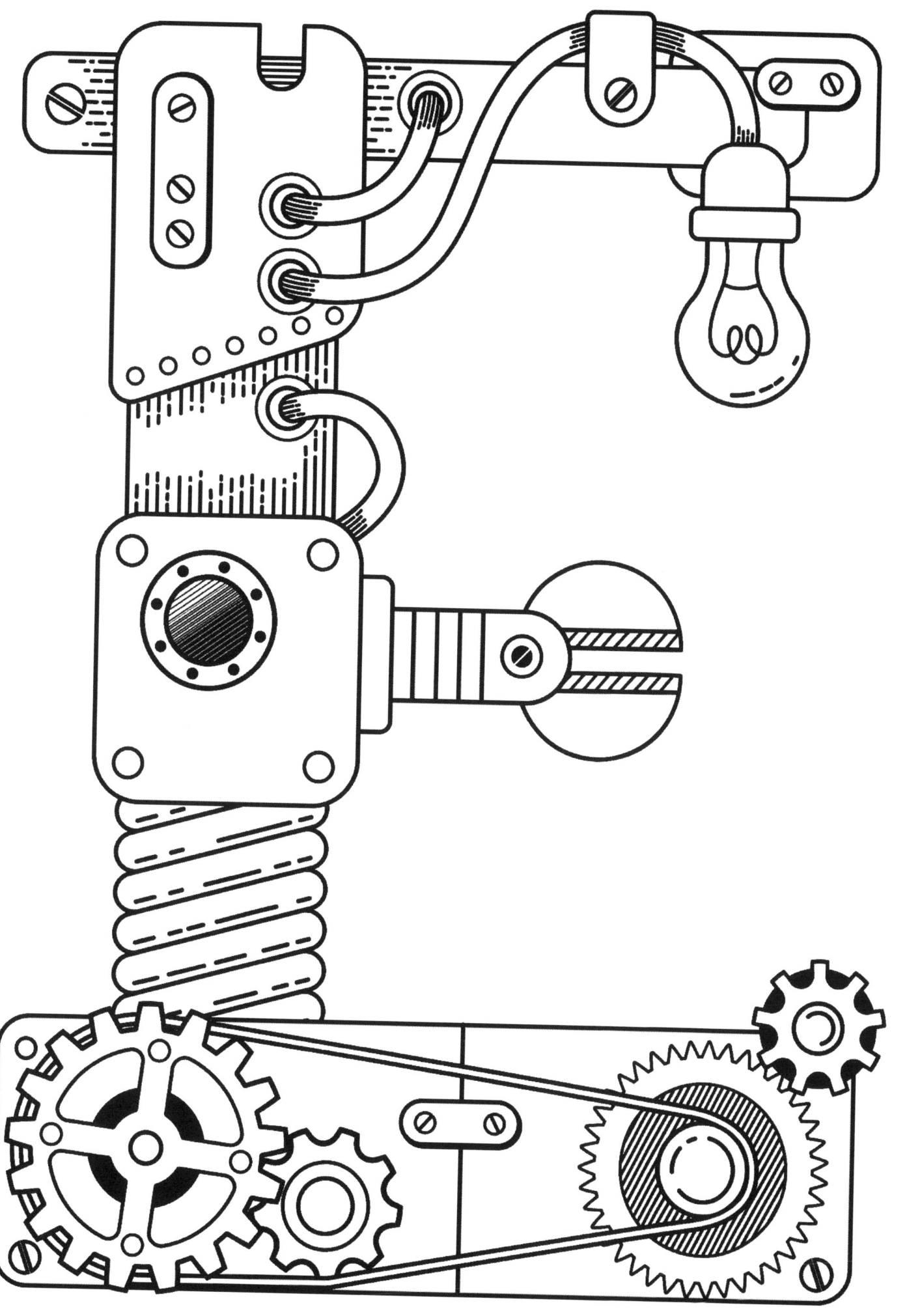

MEZZO
ZENTANGLE
DESIGNS

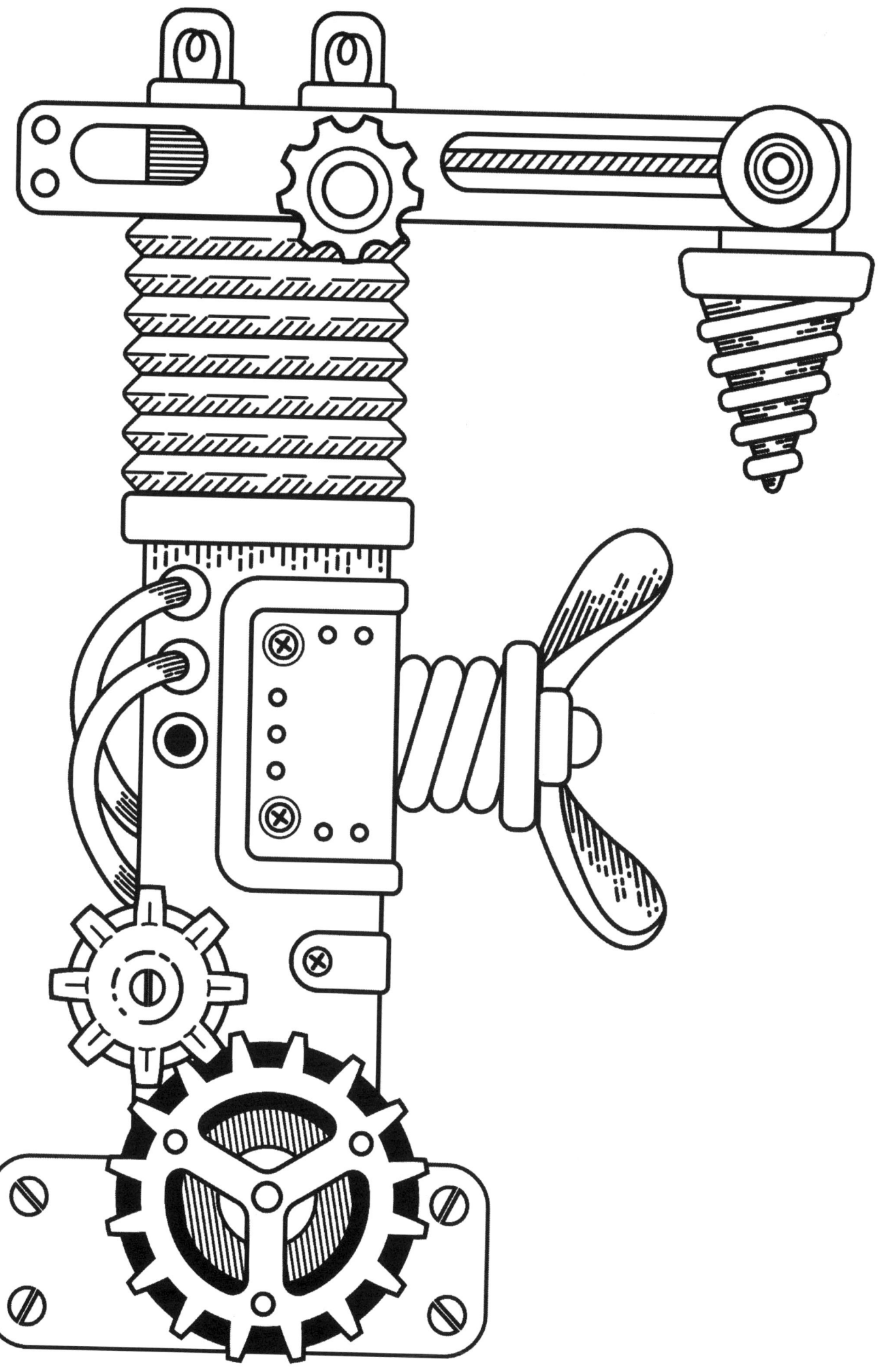

MEZZO
ZENTANGLE
DESIGNS

MEZZO
ZENTANGLE
DESIGNS

MEZZO
ZENTANGLE
DESIGNS

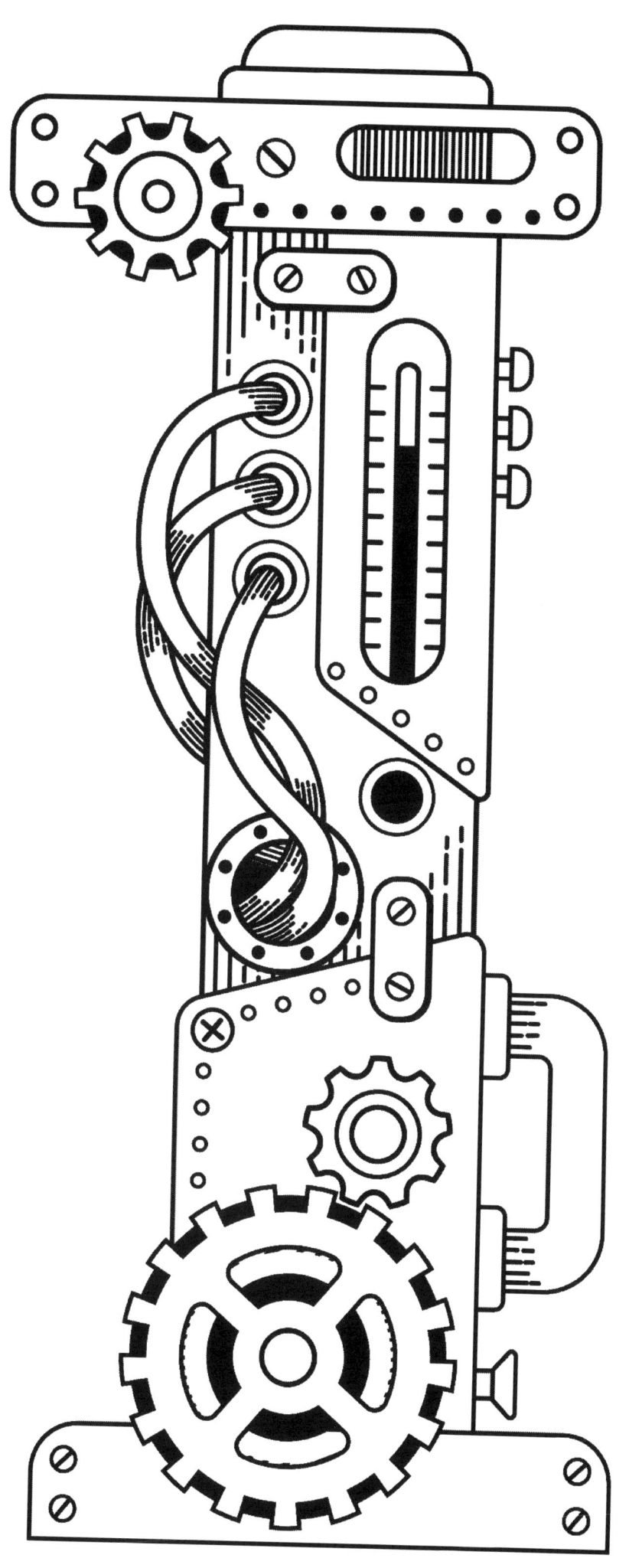

MEZZO
ZENTANGLE
DESIGNS

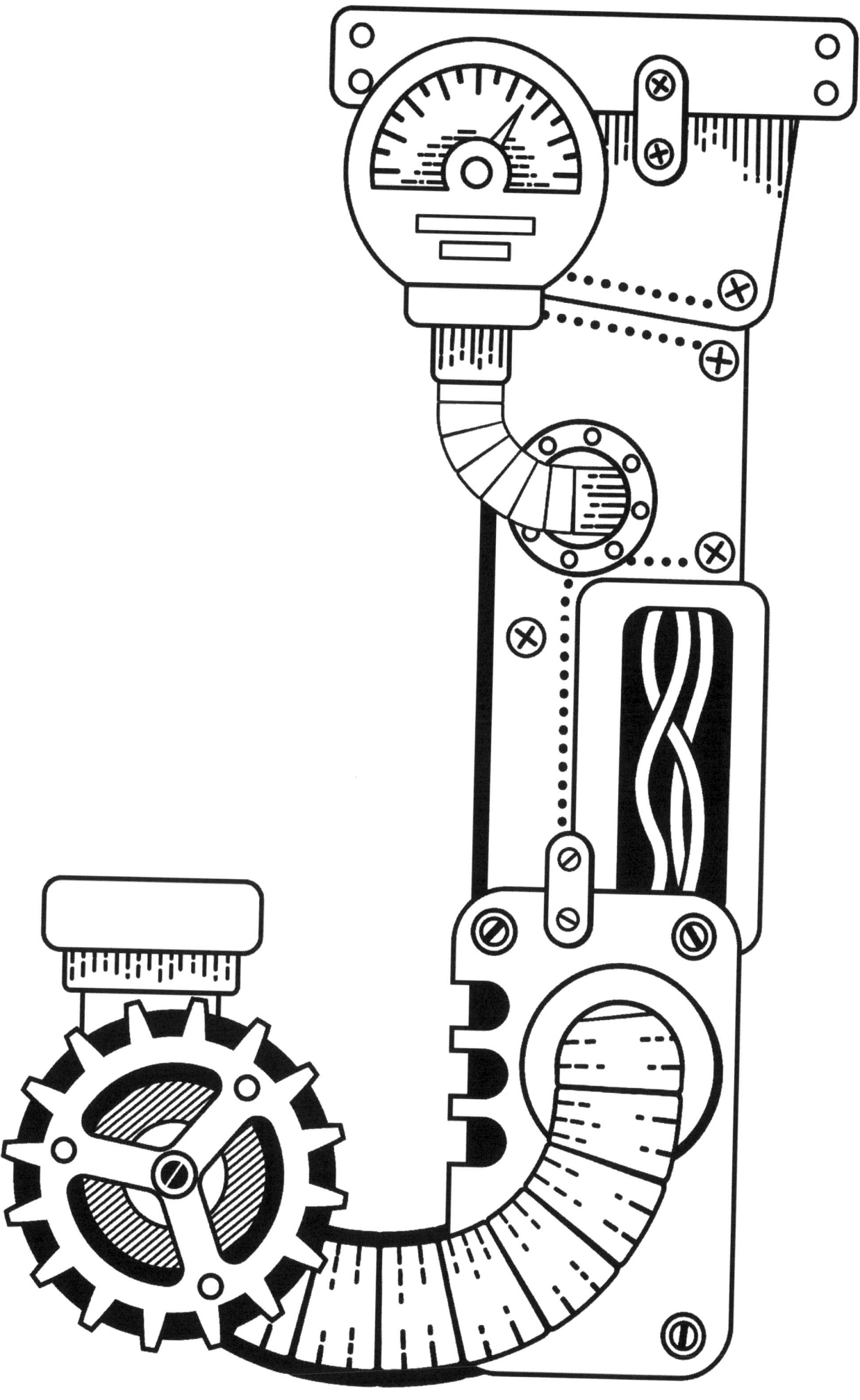

MEZZO
ZENTANGLE
DESIGNS

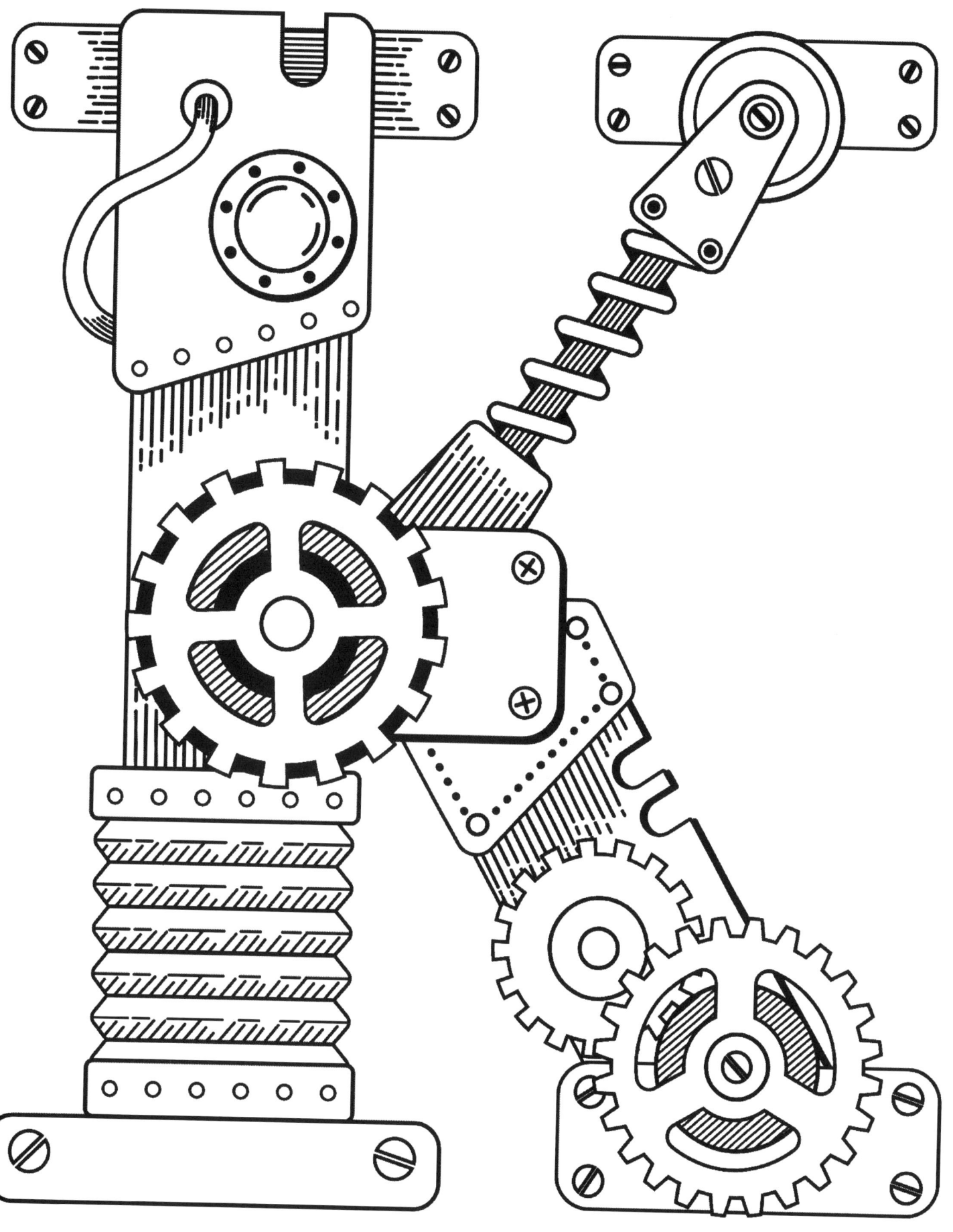

MEZZO
ZENTANGLE
DESIGNS

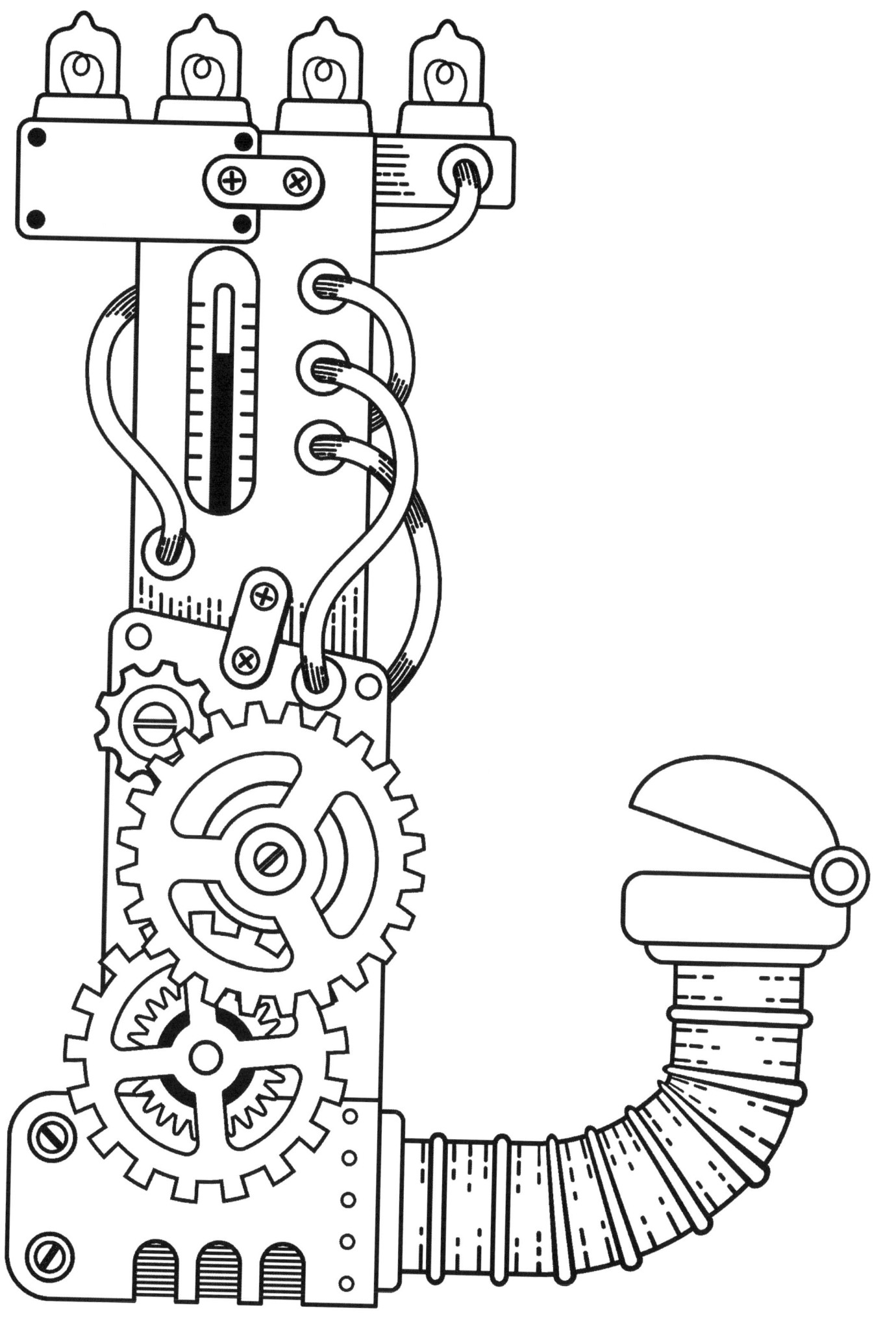

MEZZO
ZENTANGLE
DESIGNS

MEZZO
ZENTANGLE
DESIGNS

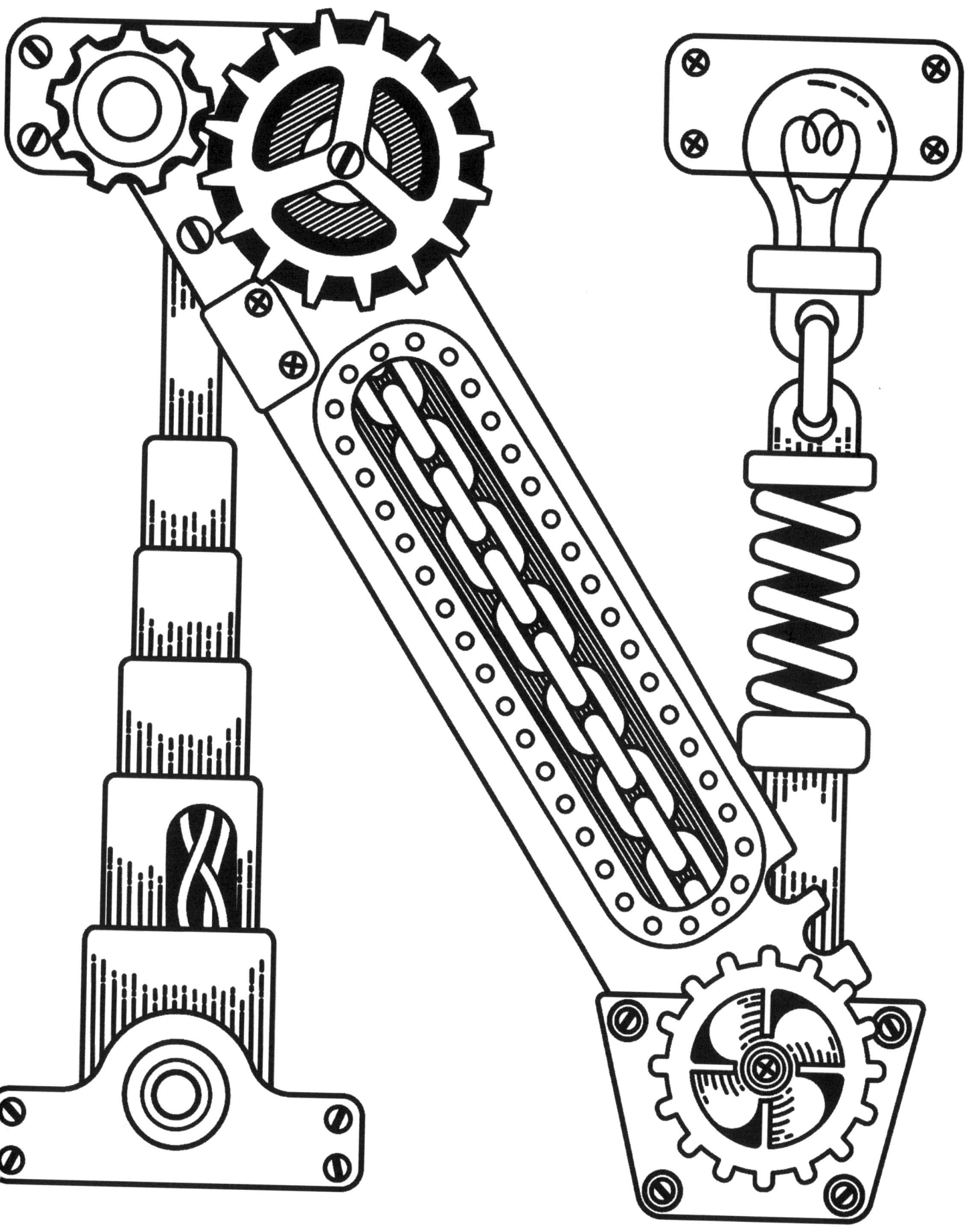

MEZZO
ZENTANGLE
DESIGNS

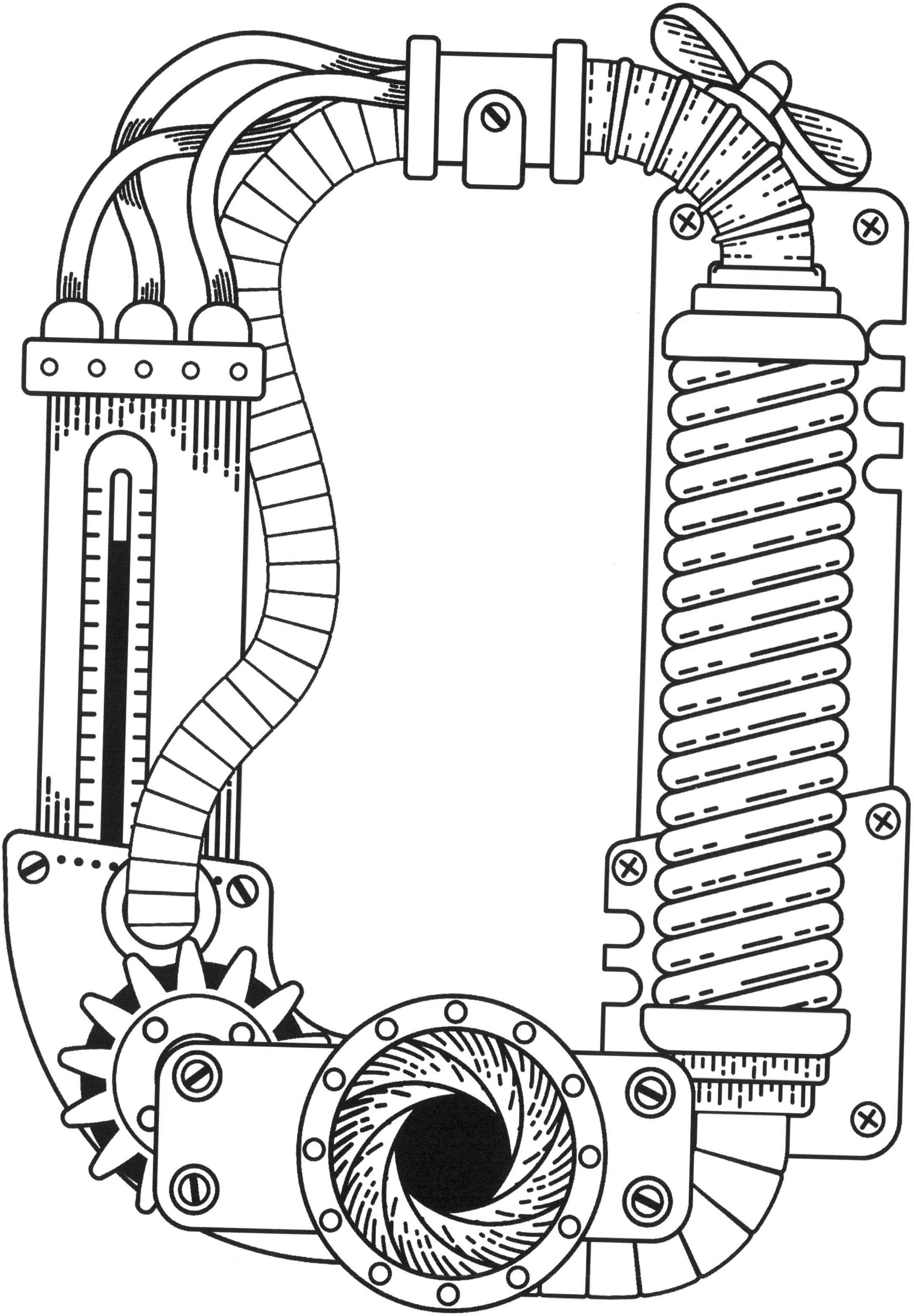

MEZZO
ZENTANGLE
DESIGNS

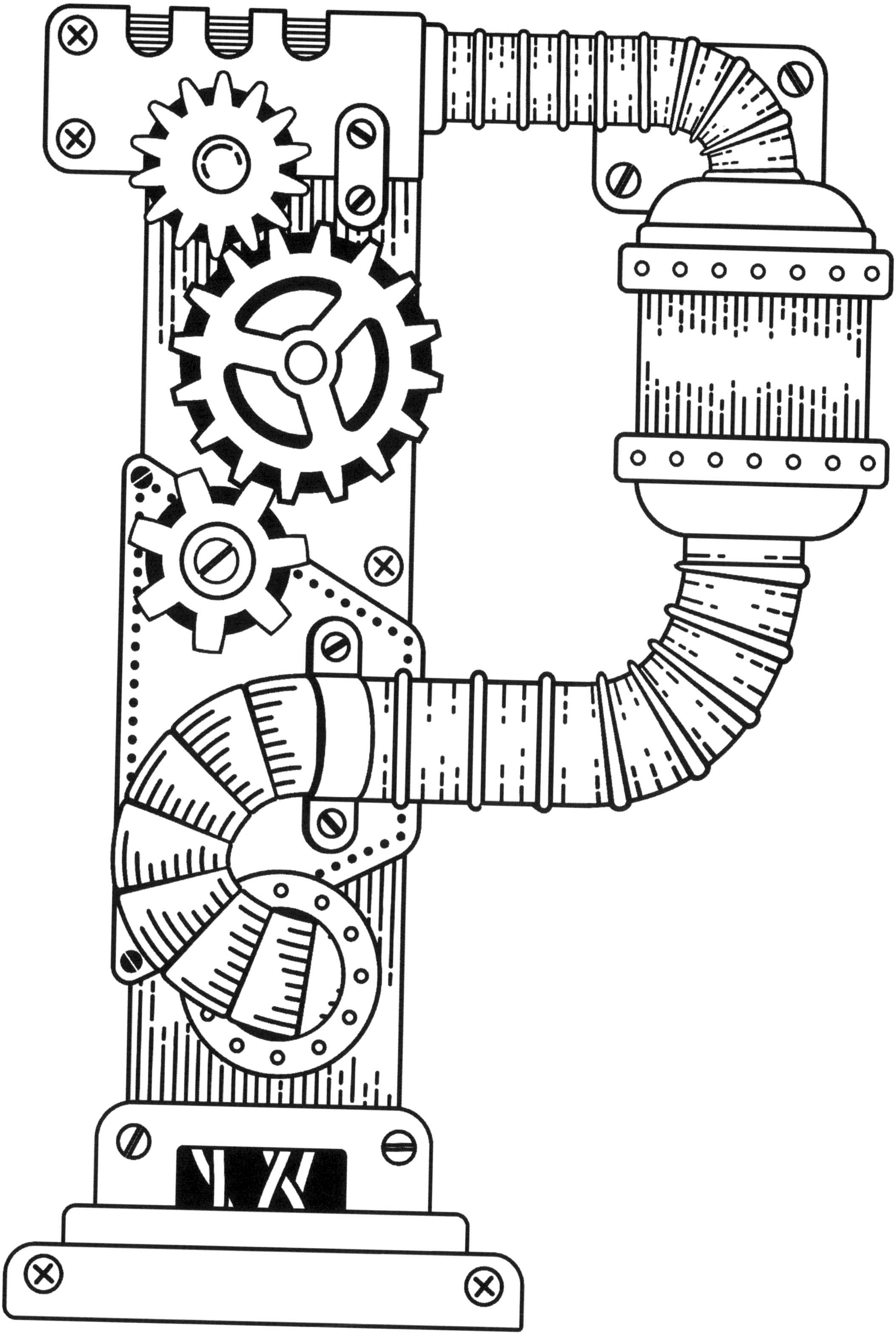

MEZZO
ZENTANGLE
DESIGNS

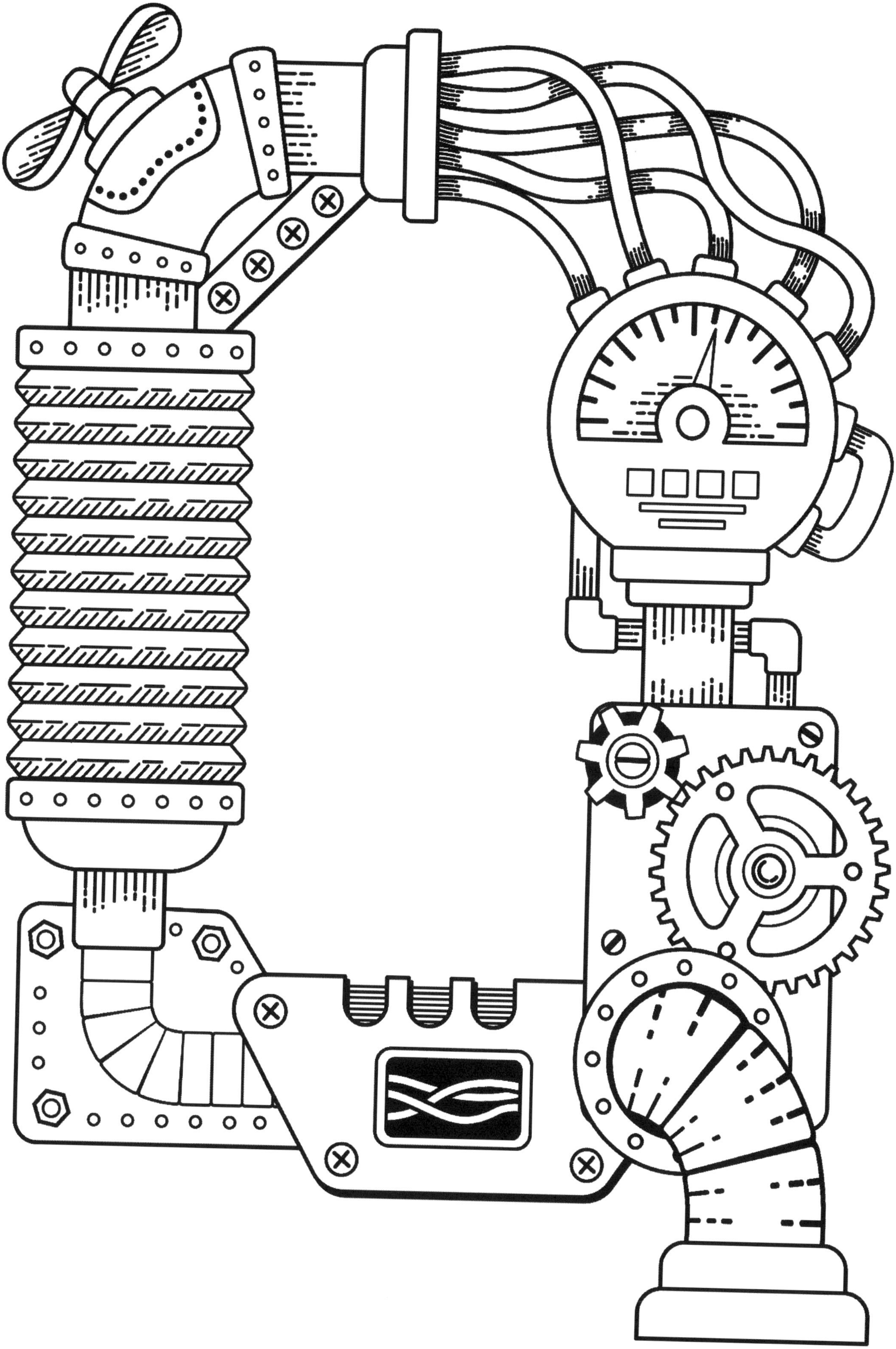

MEZZO
ZENTANGLE
DESIGNS

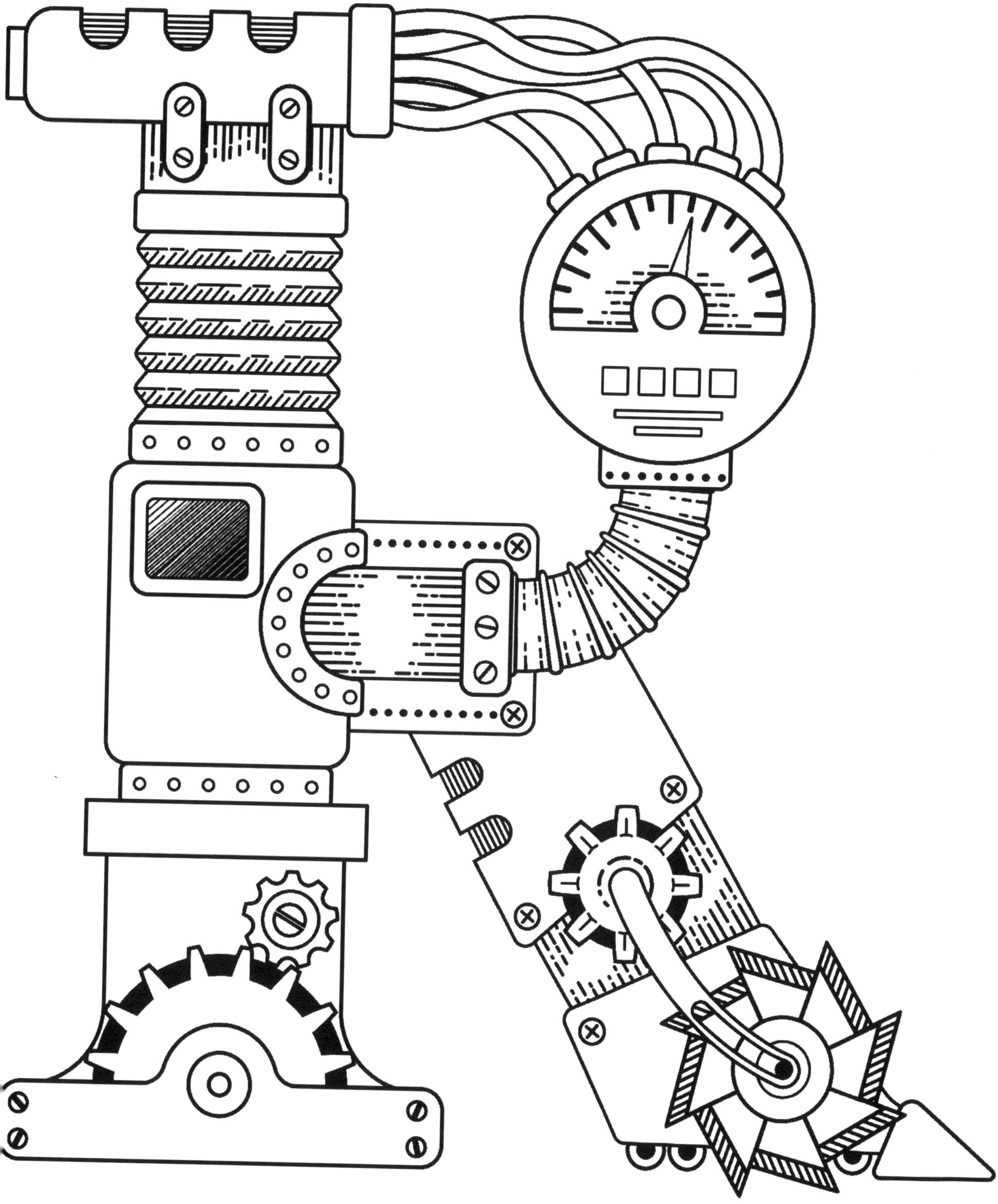

MEZZO
ZENTANGLE
DESIGNS

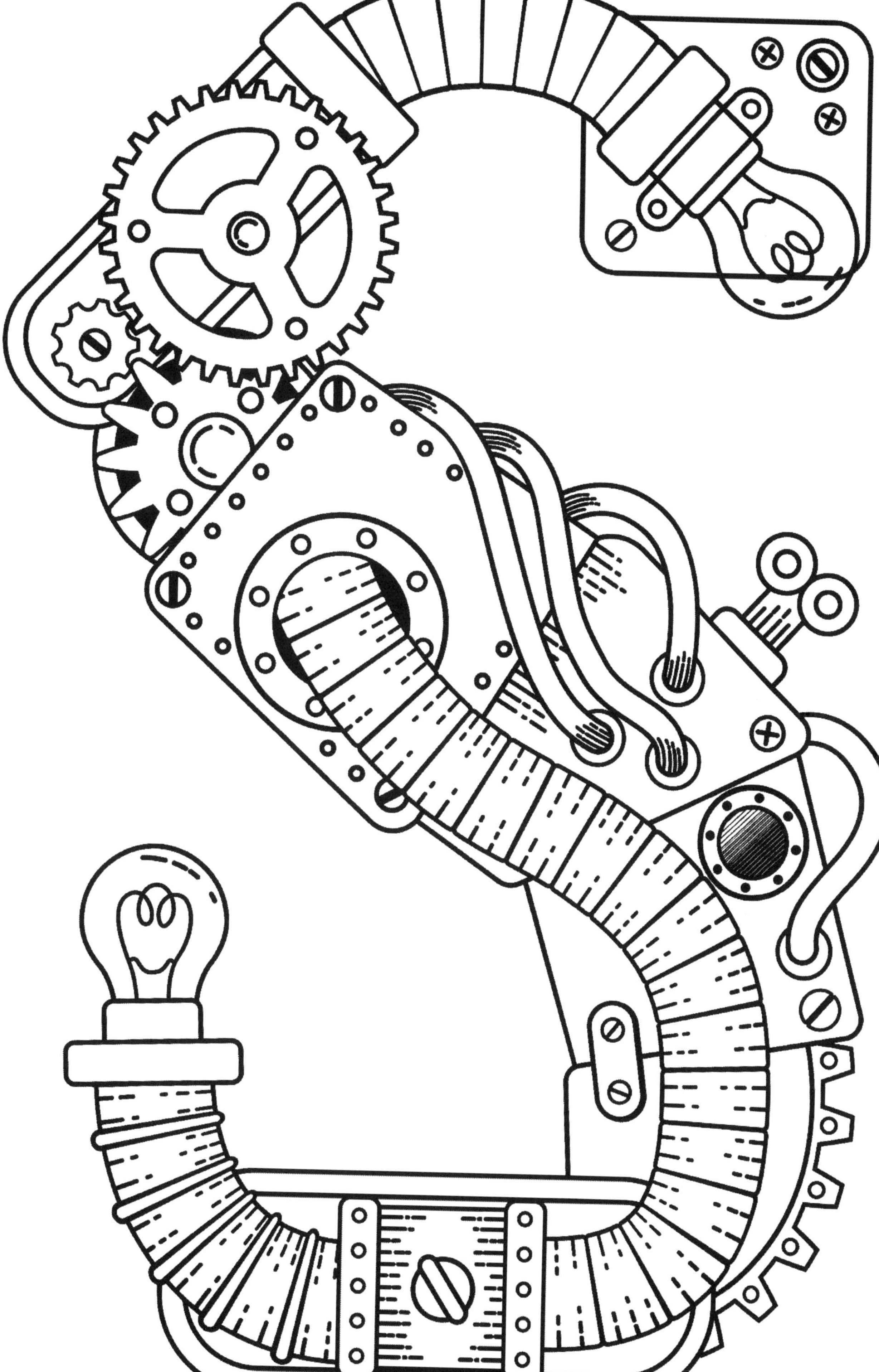

MEZZO
ZENTANGLE
DESIGNS

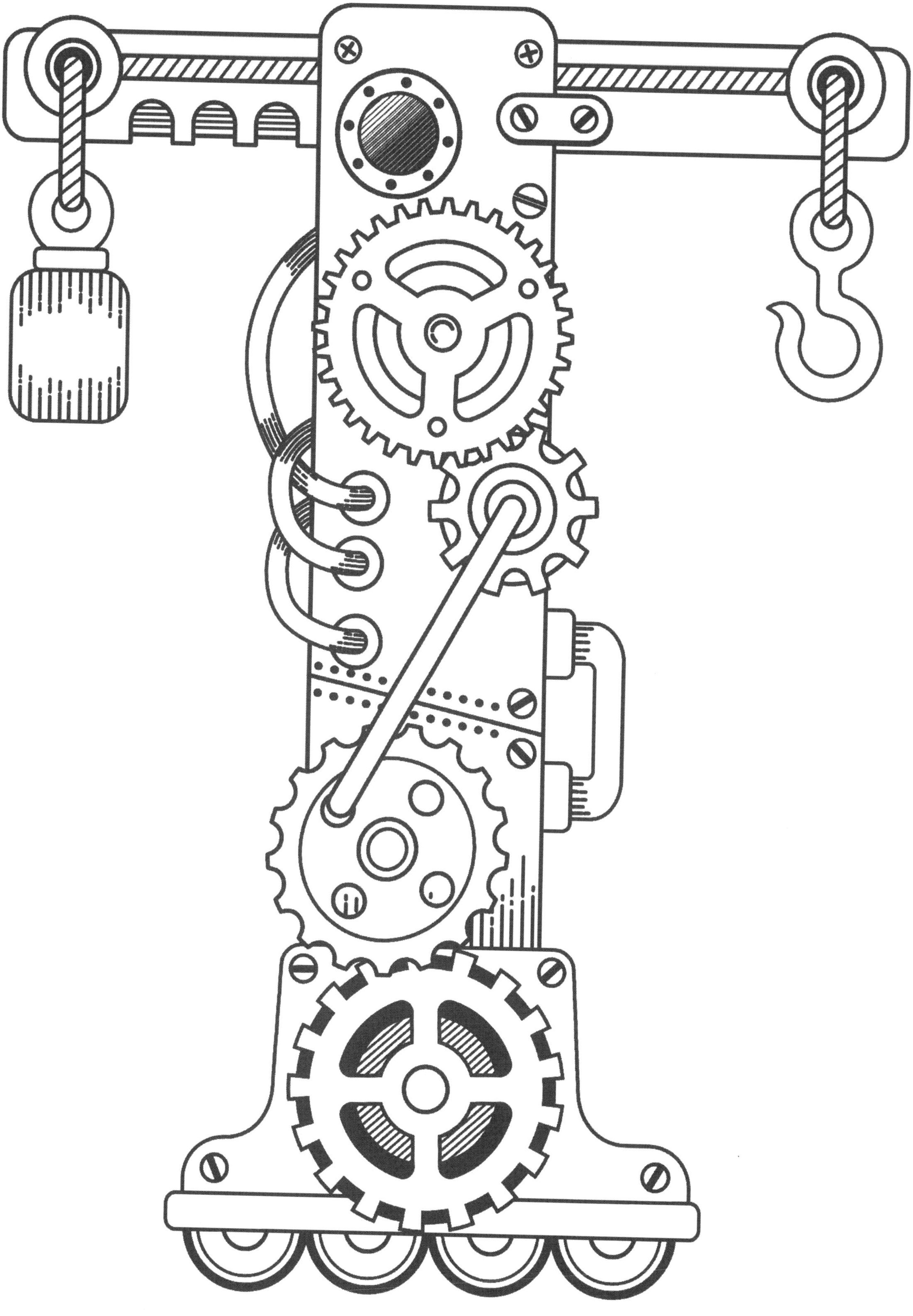

MEZZO
ZENTANGLE
DESIGNS

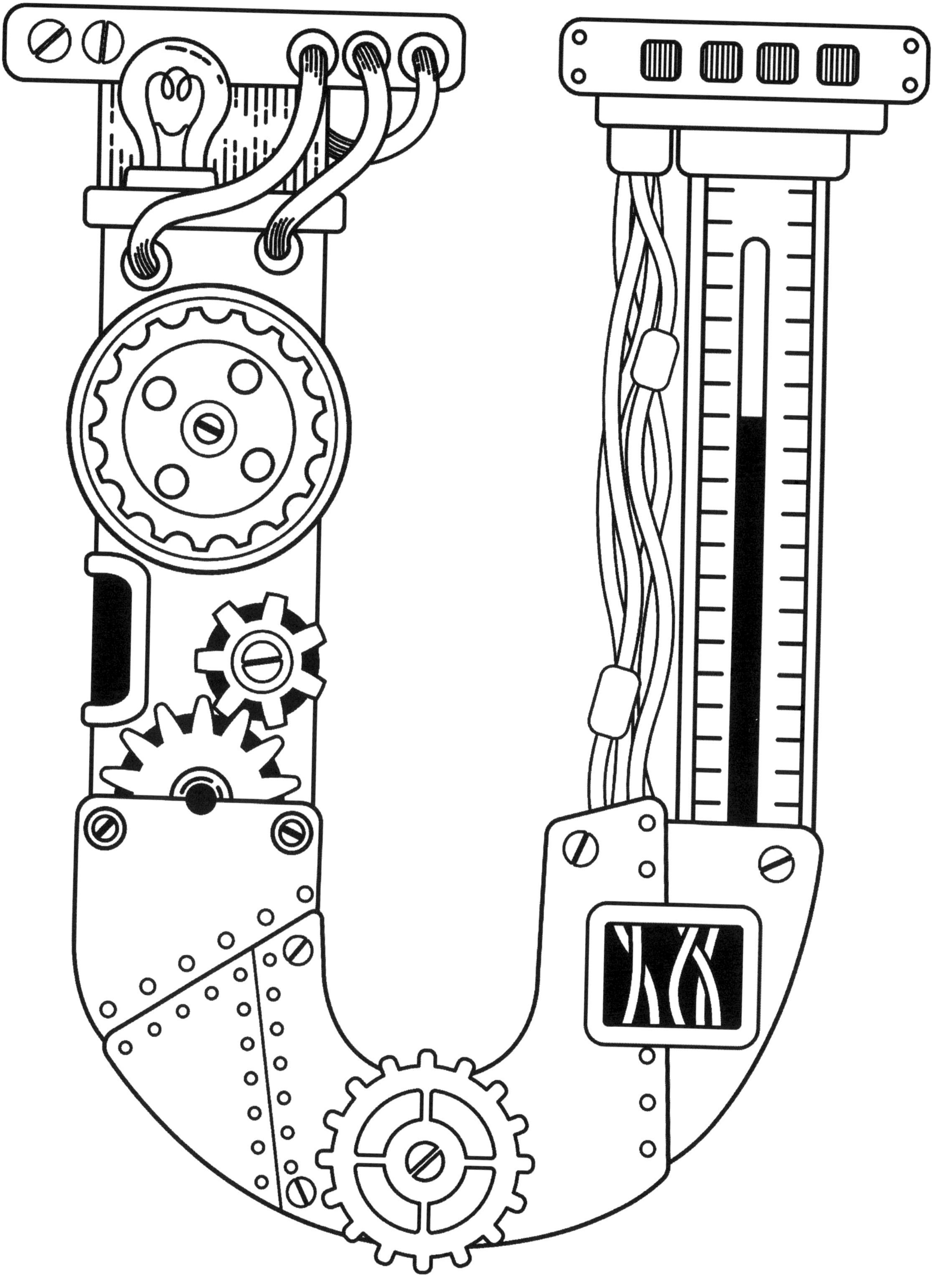

MEZZO
ZENTANGLE
DESIGNS

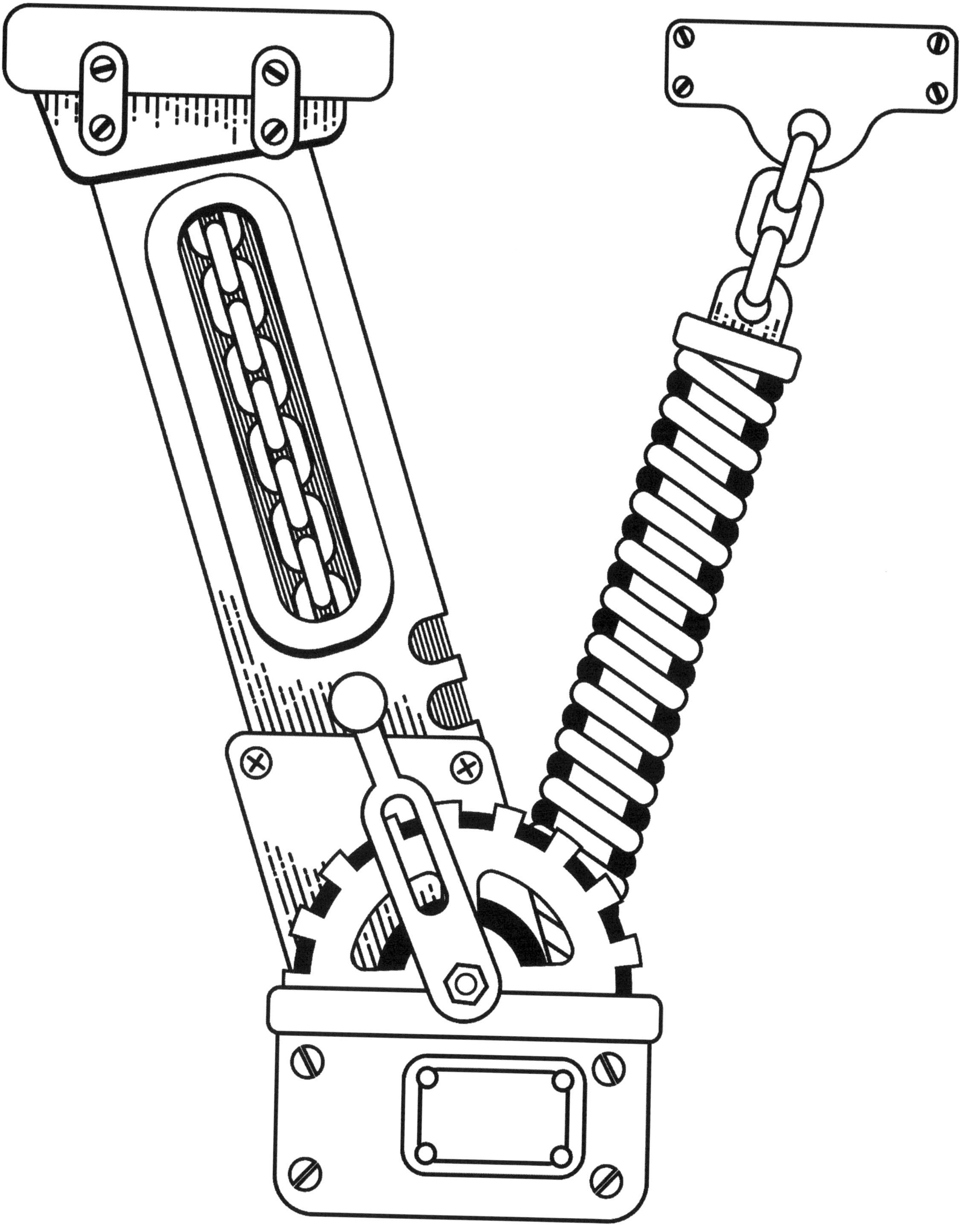

MEZZO
ZENTANGLE
DESIGNS

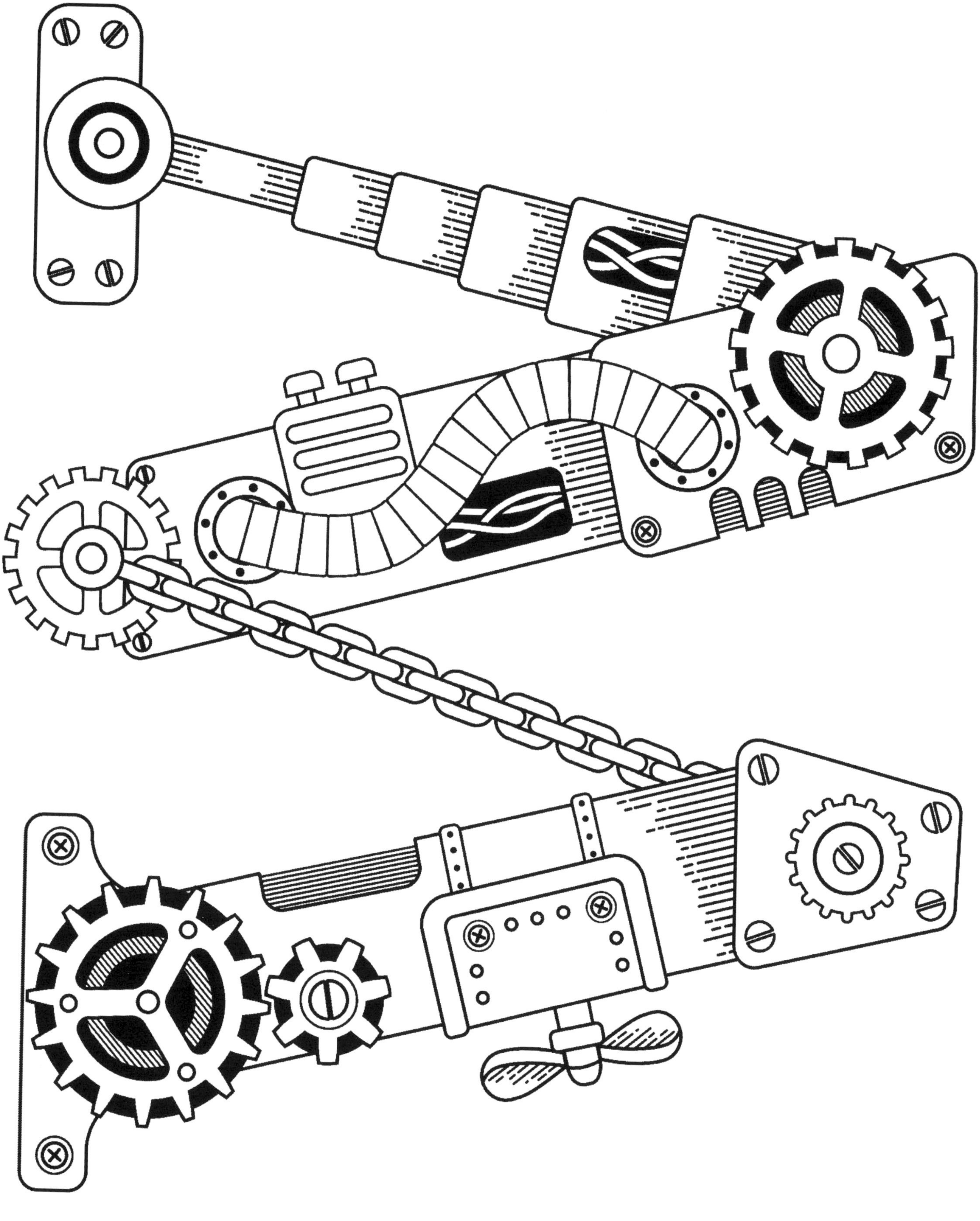

MEZZO
ZENTANGLE
DESIGNS

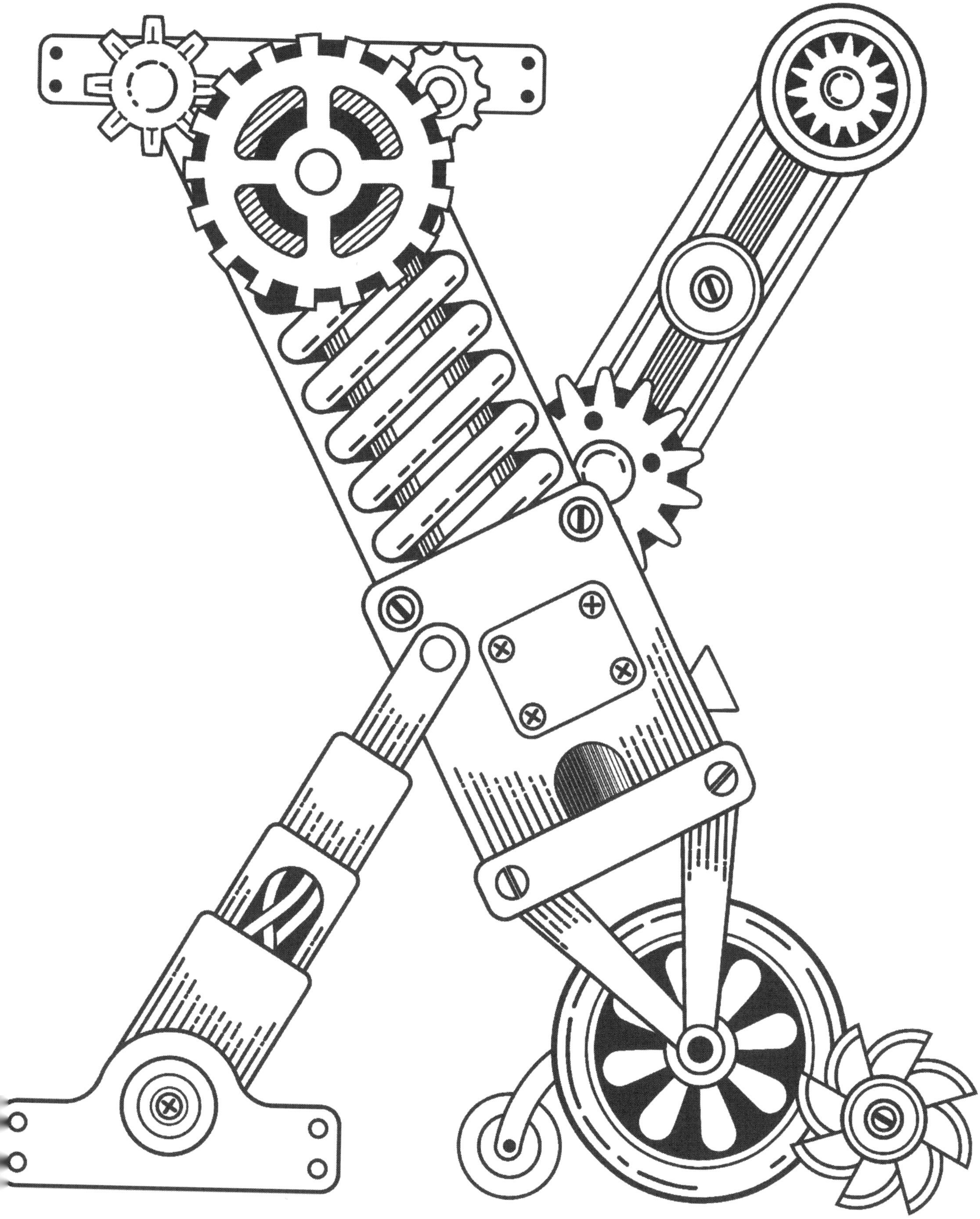

MEZZO
ZENTANGLE
DESIGNS

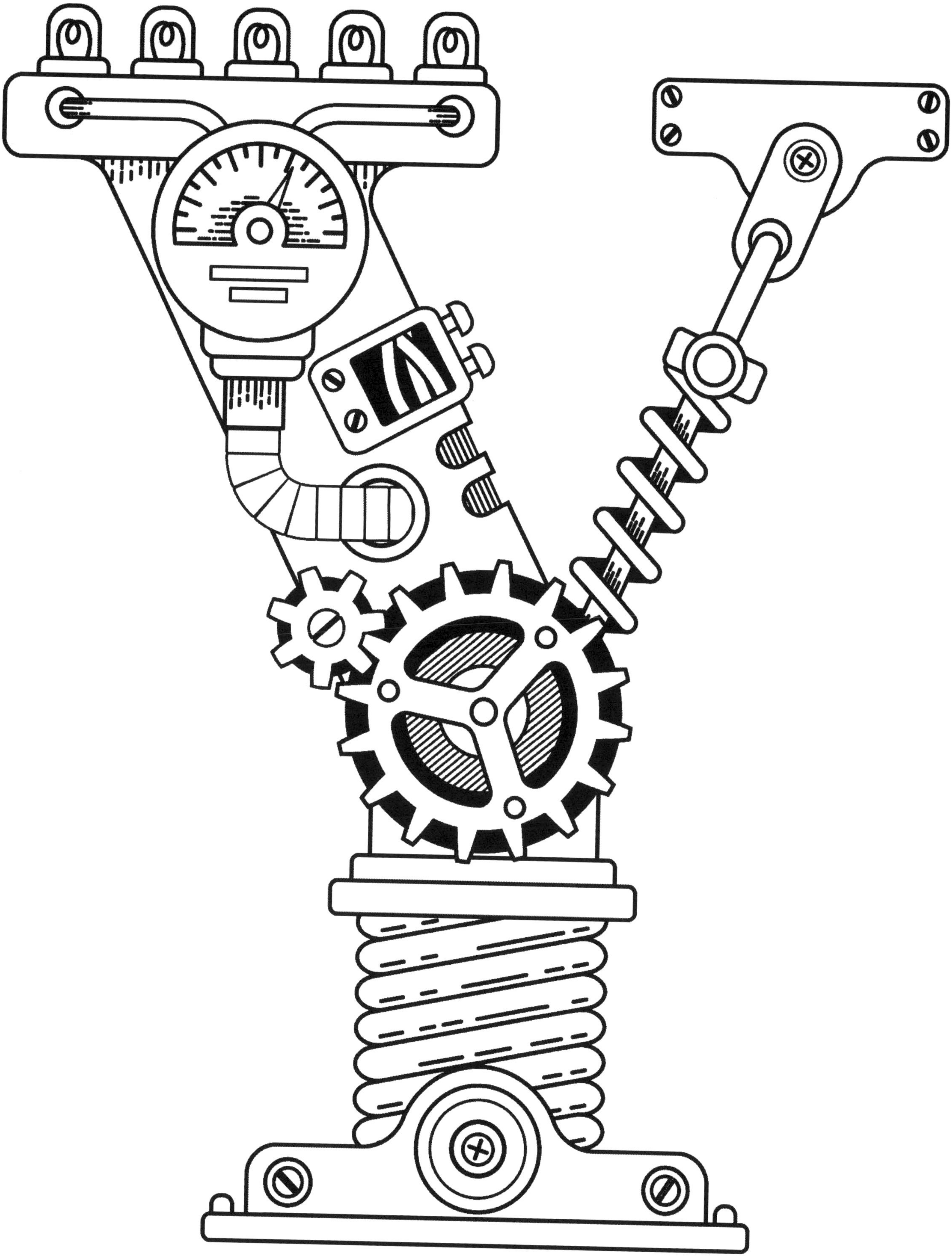

MEZZO
ZENTANGLE
DESIGNS

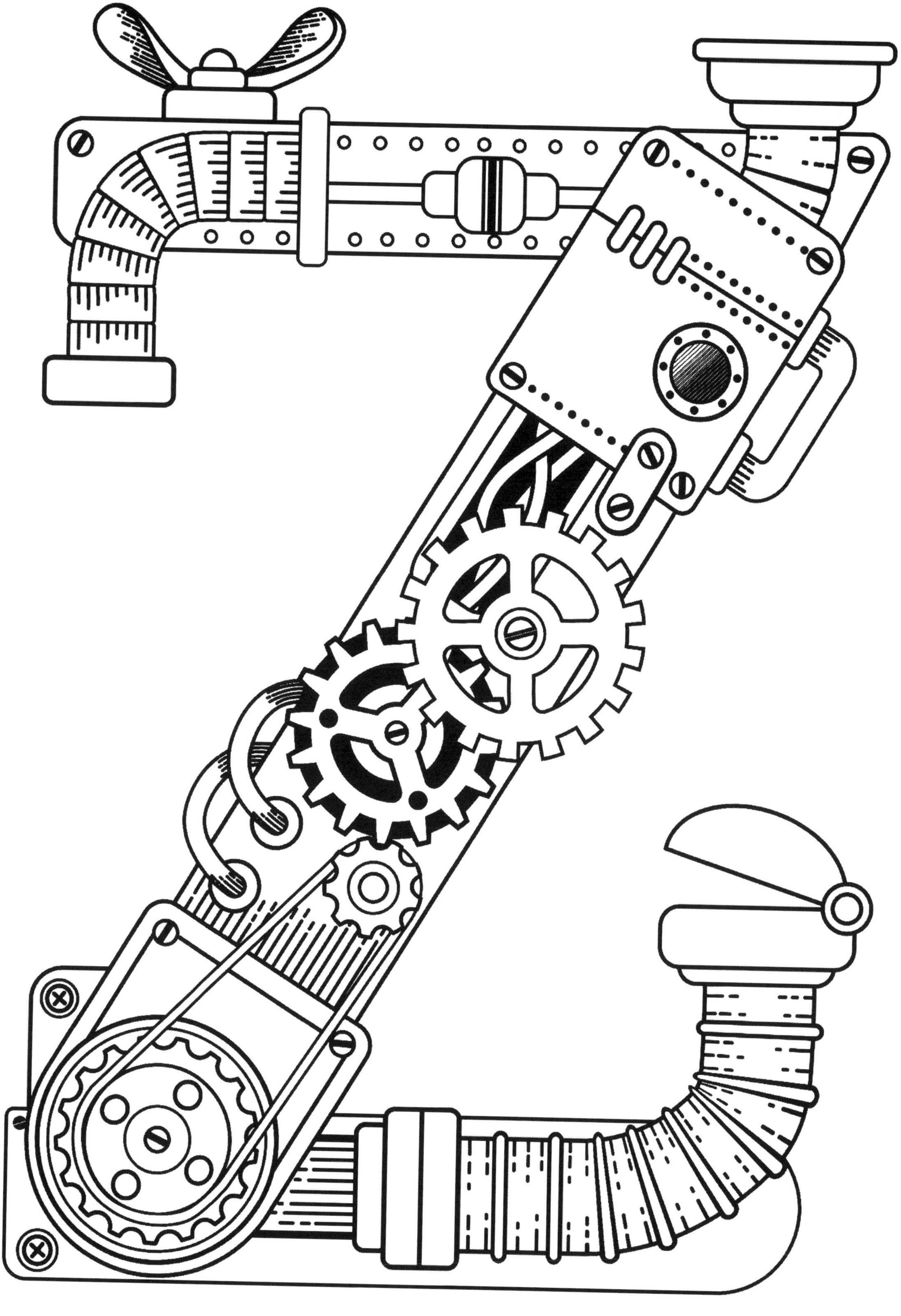

MEZZO
ZENTANGLE
DESIGNS

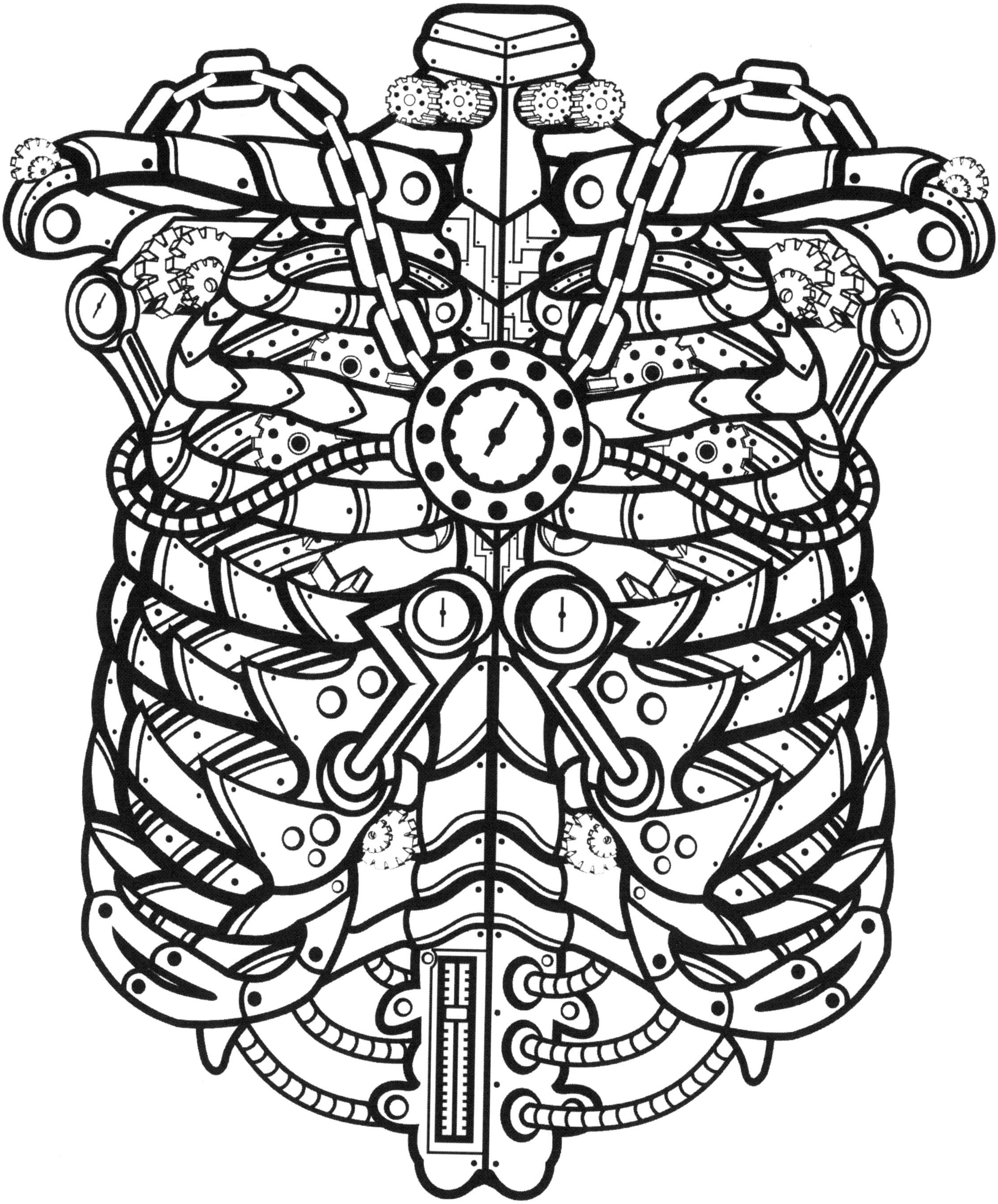

MEZZO
ZENTANGLE
DESIGNS

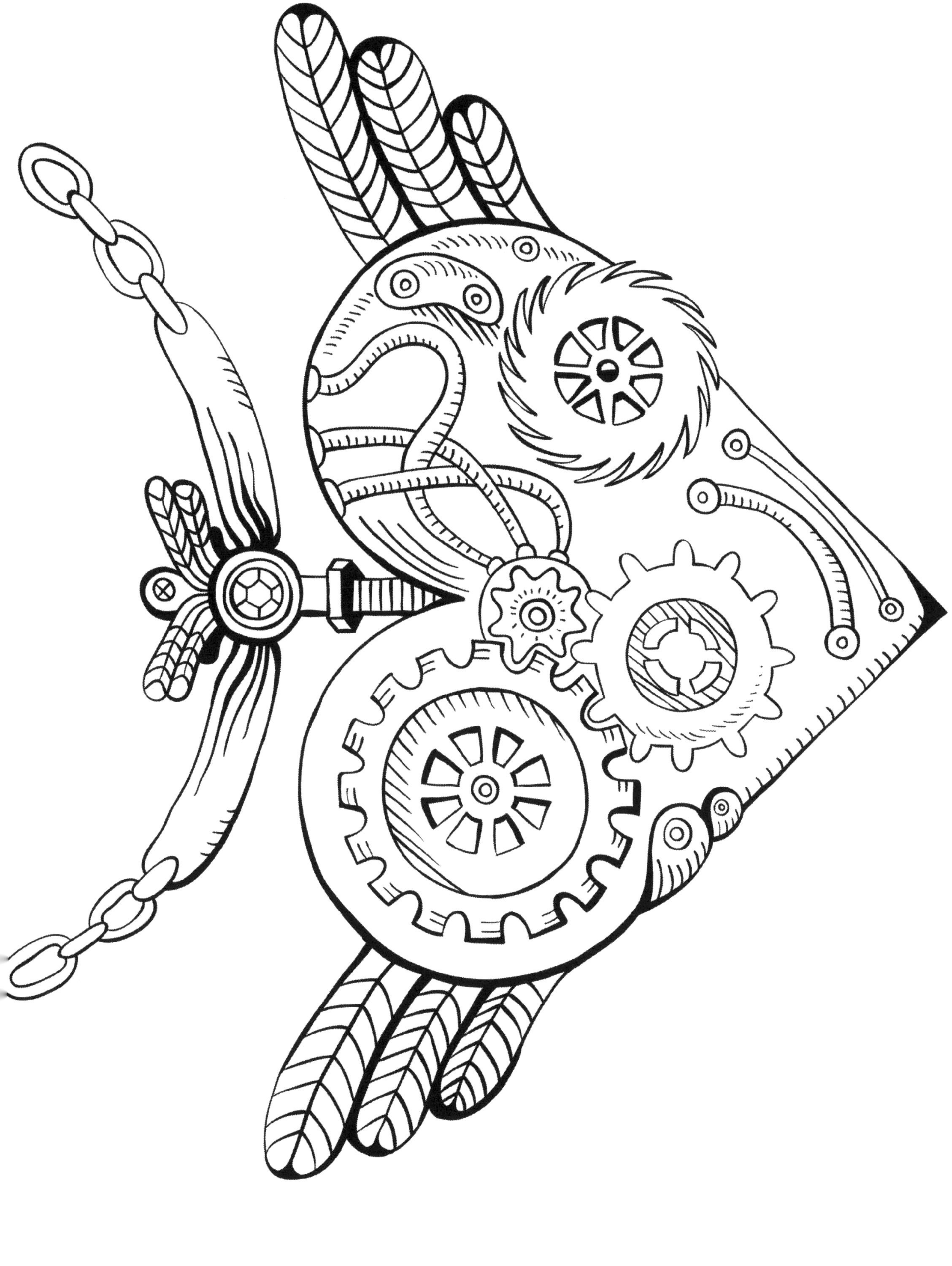

MEZZO ZENTANGLE DESIGNS

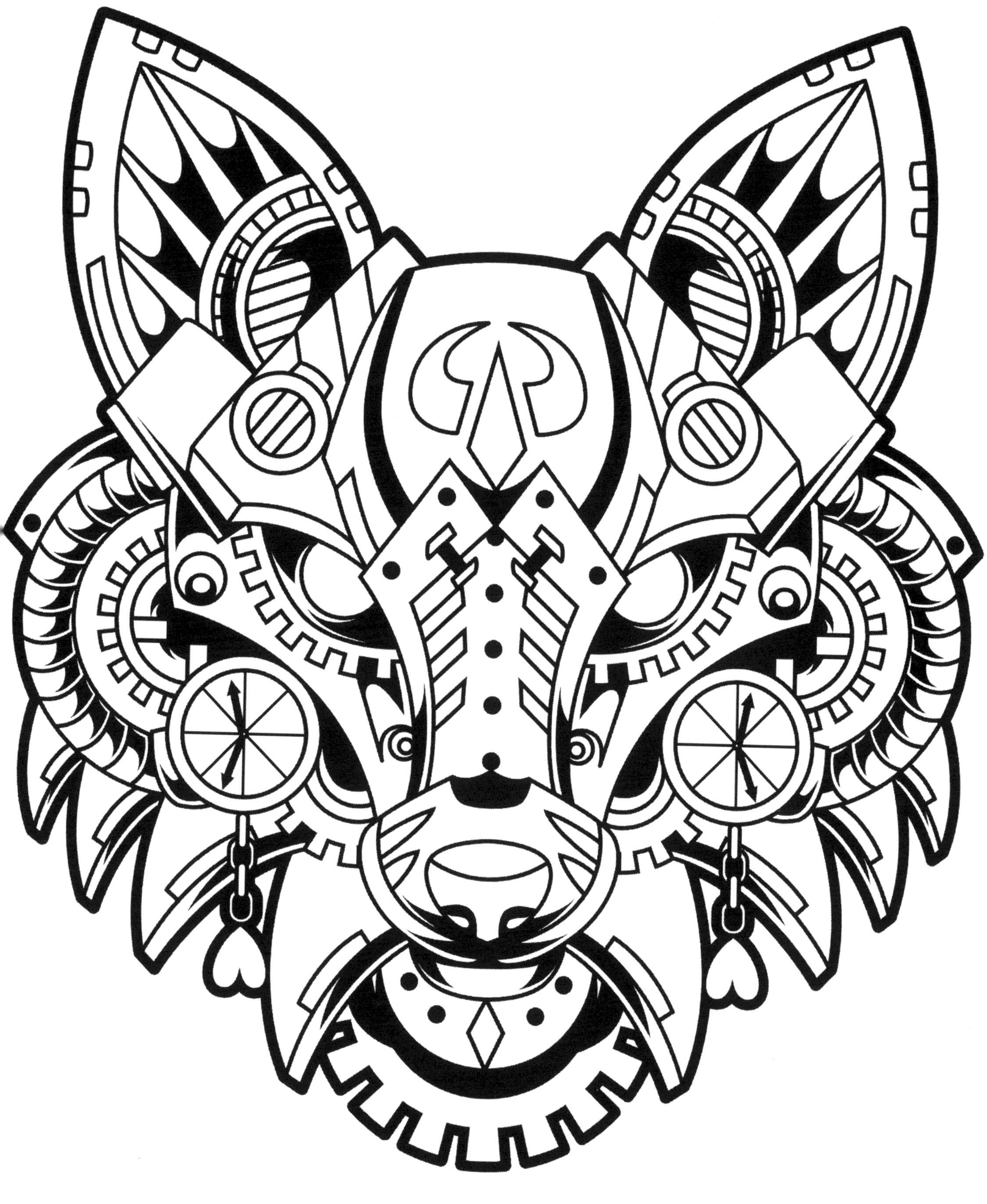

MEZZO
ZENTANGLE
DESIGNS

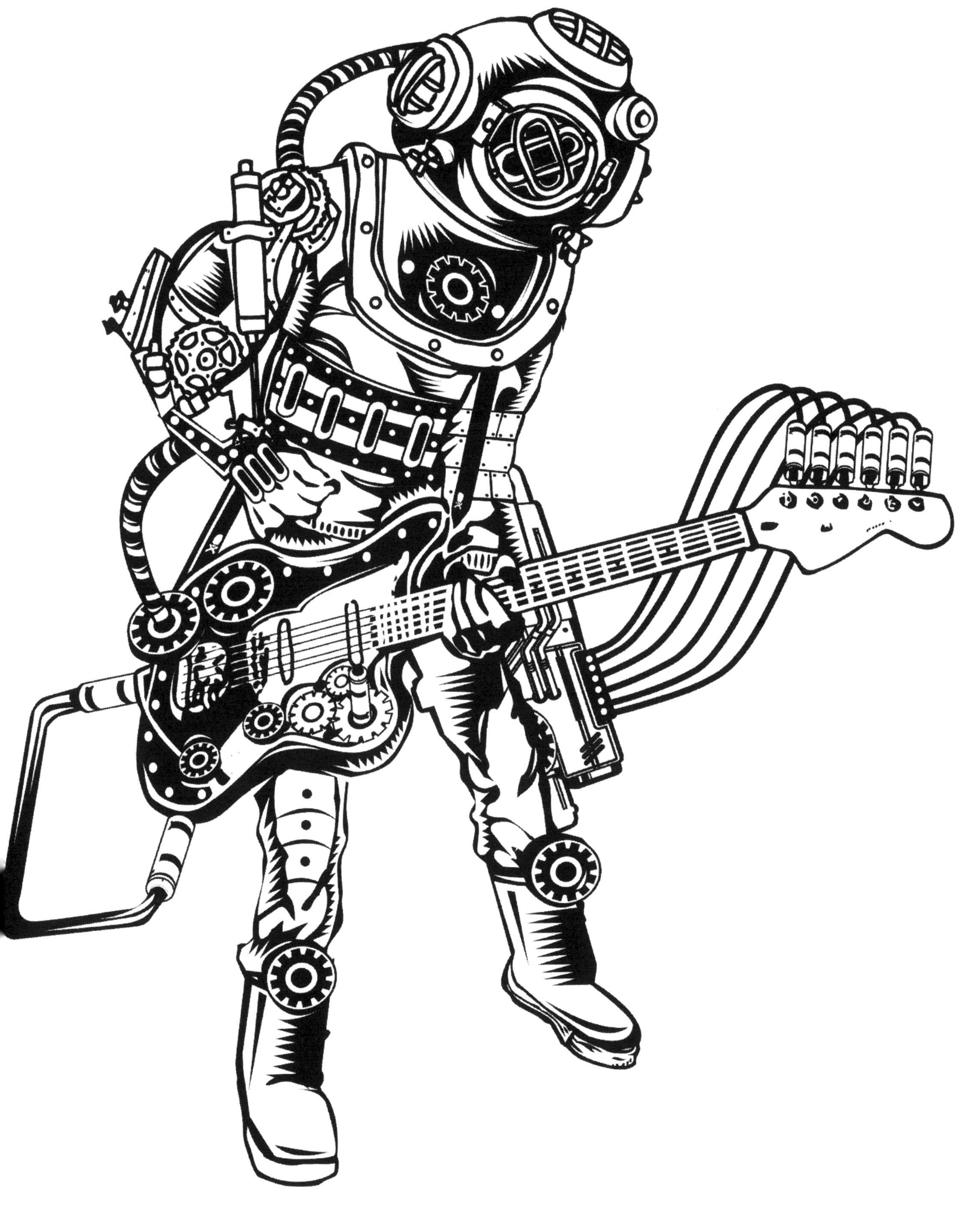

MEZZO
ZENTANGLE
DESIGNS

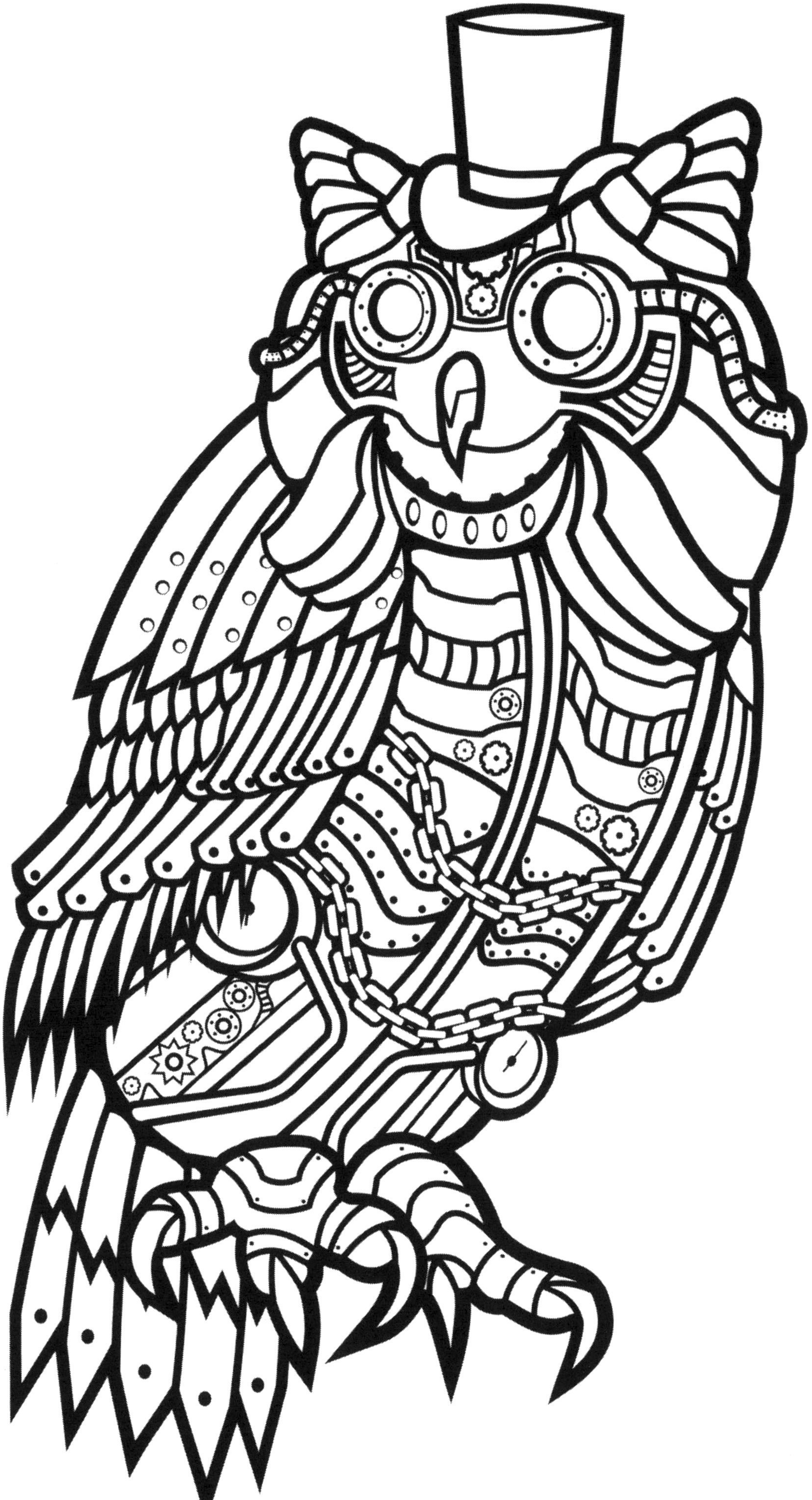

MEZZO
ZENTANGLE
DESIGNS

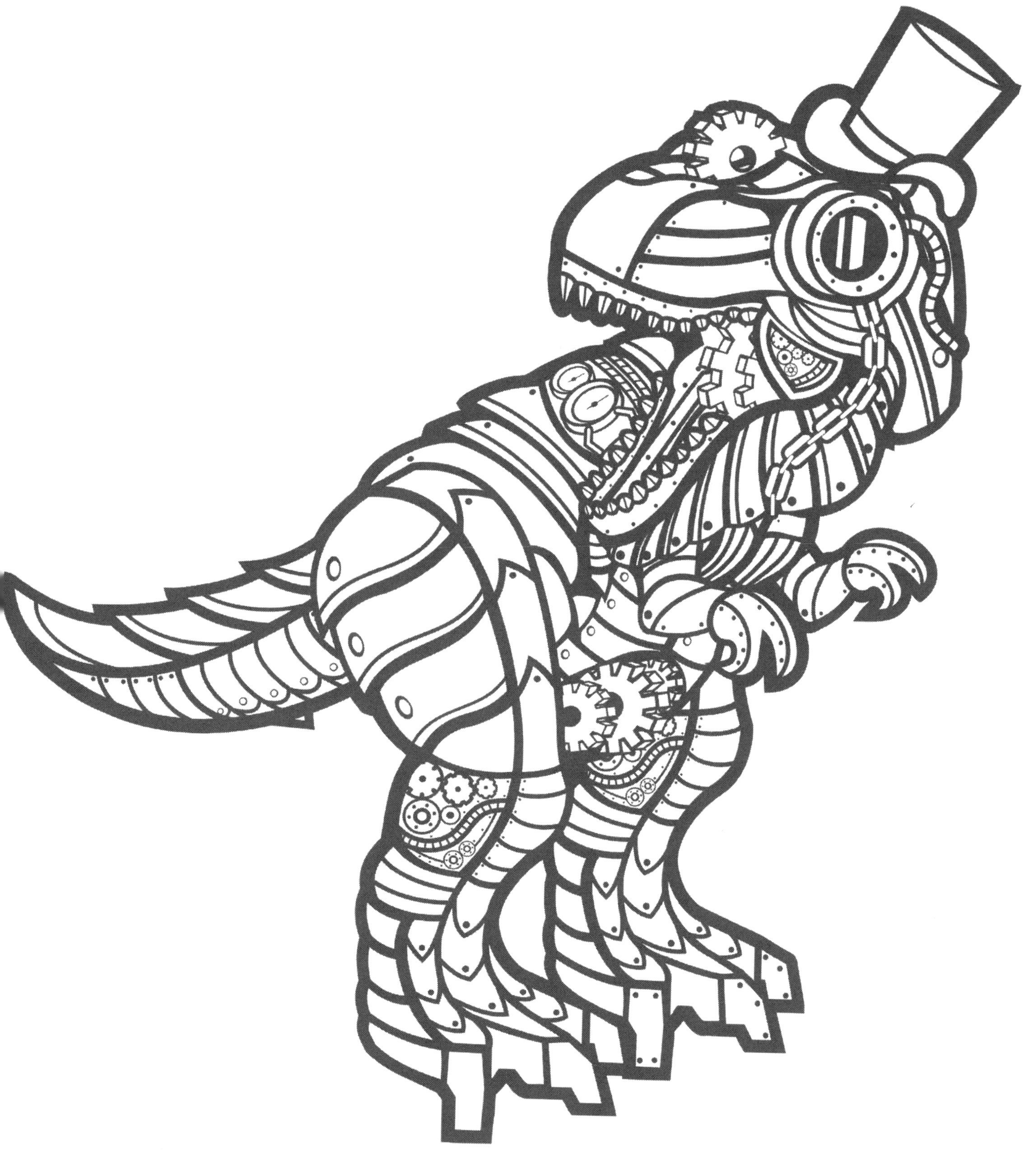

MEZZO
ZENTANGLE
DESIGNS

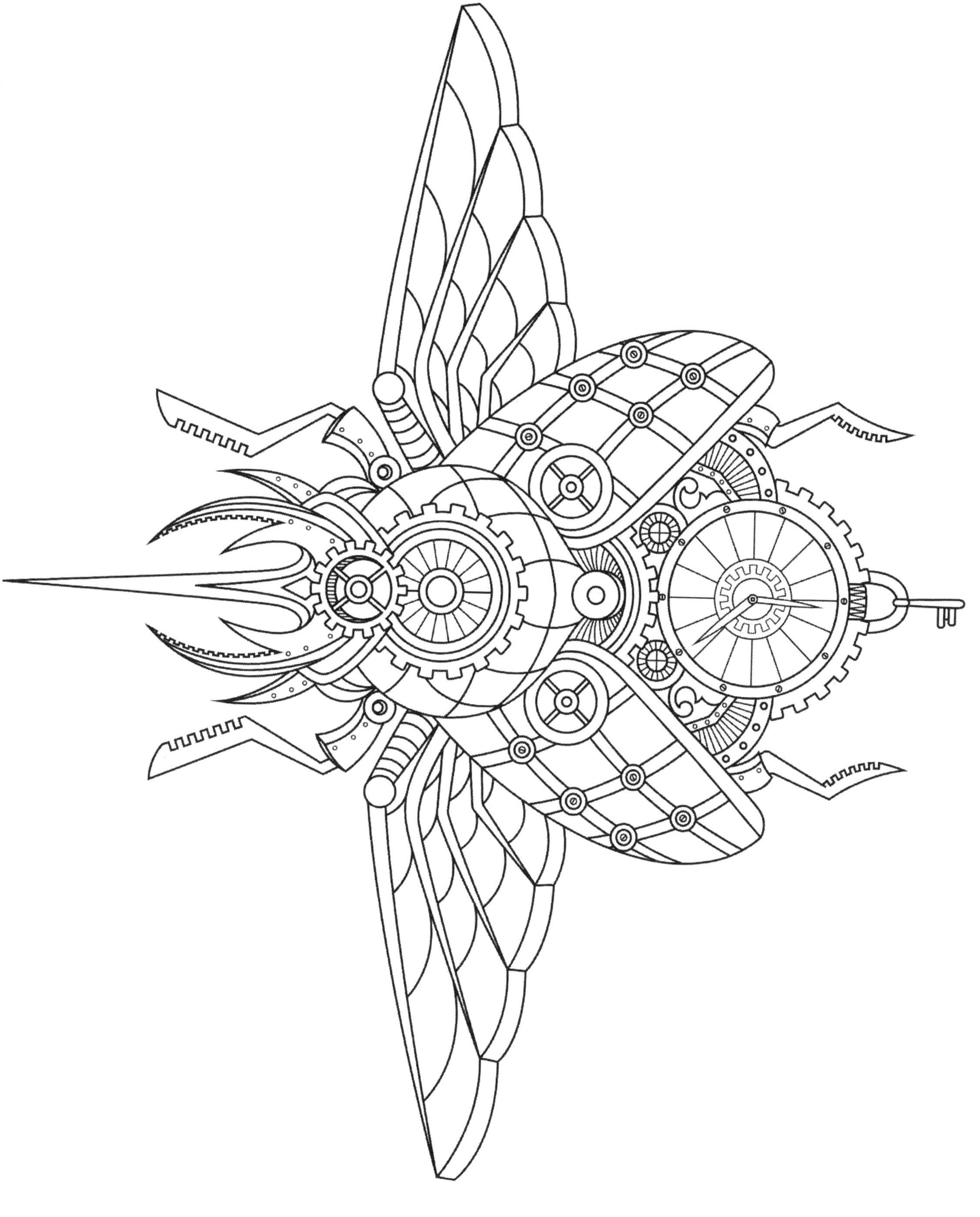

MEZZO
ZENTANGLE
DESIGNS

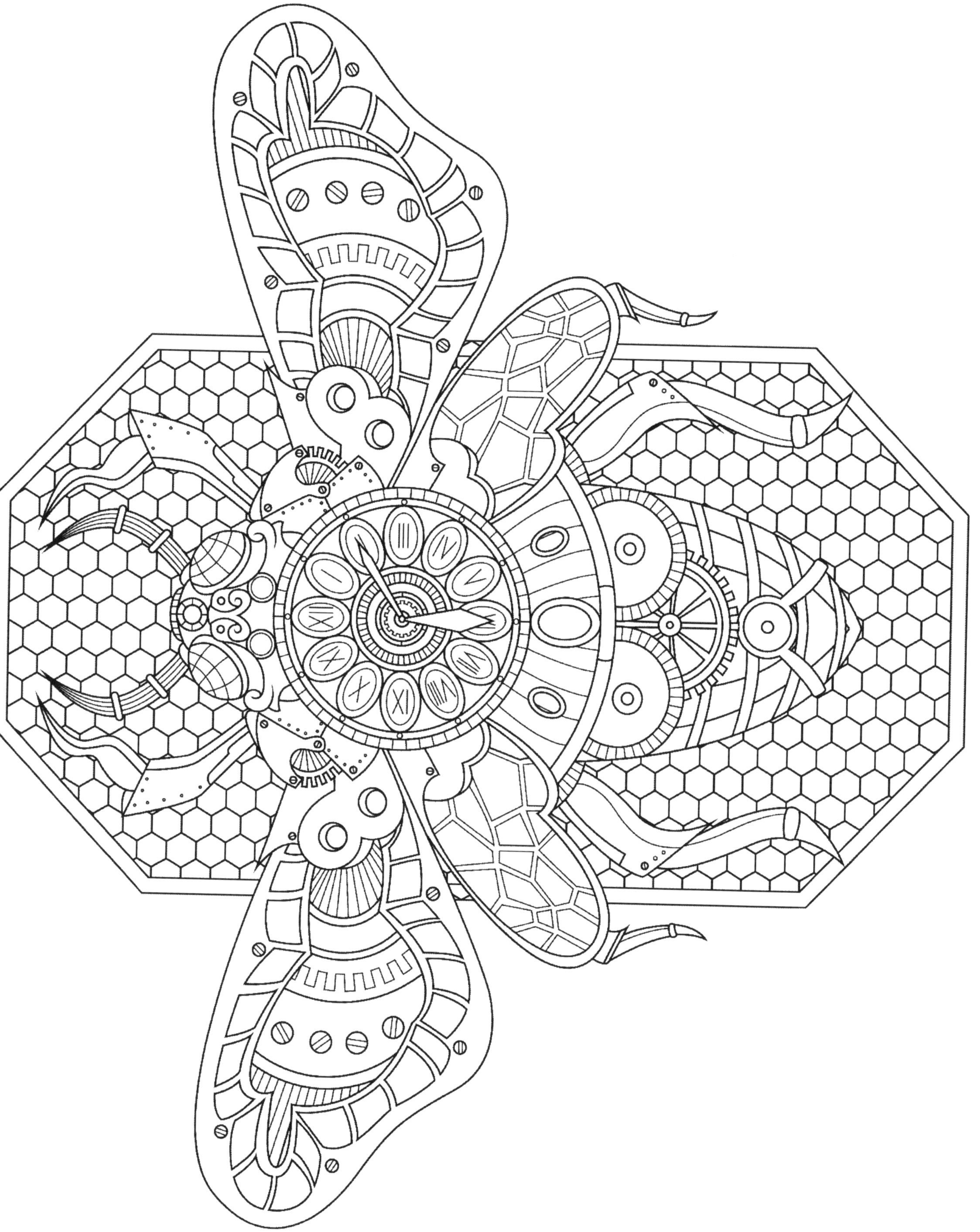

MEZZO
ZENTANGLE
DESIGNS

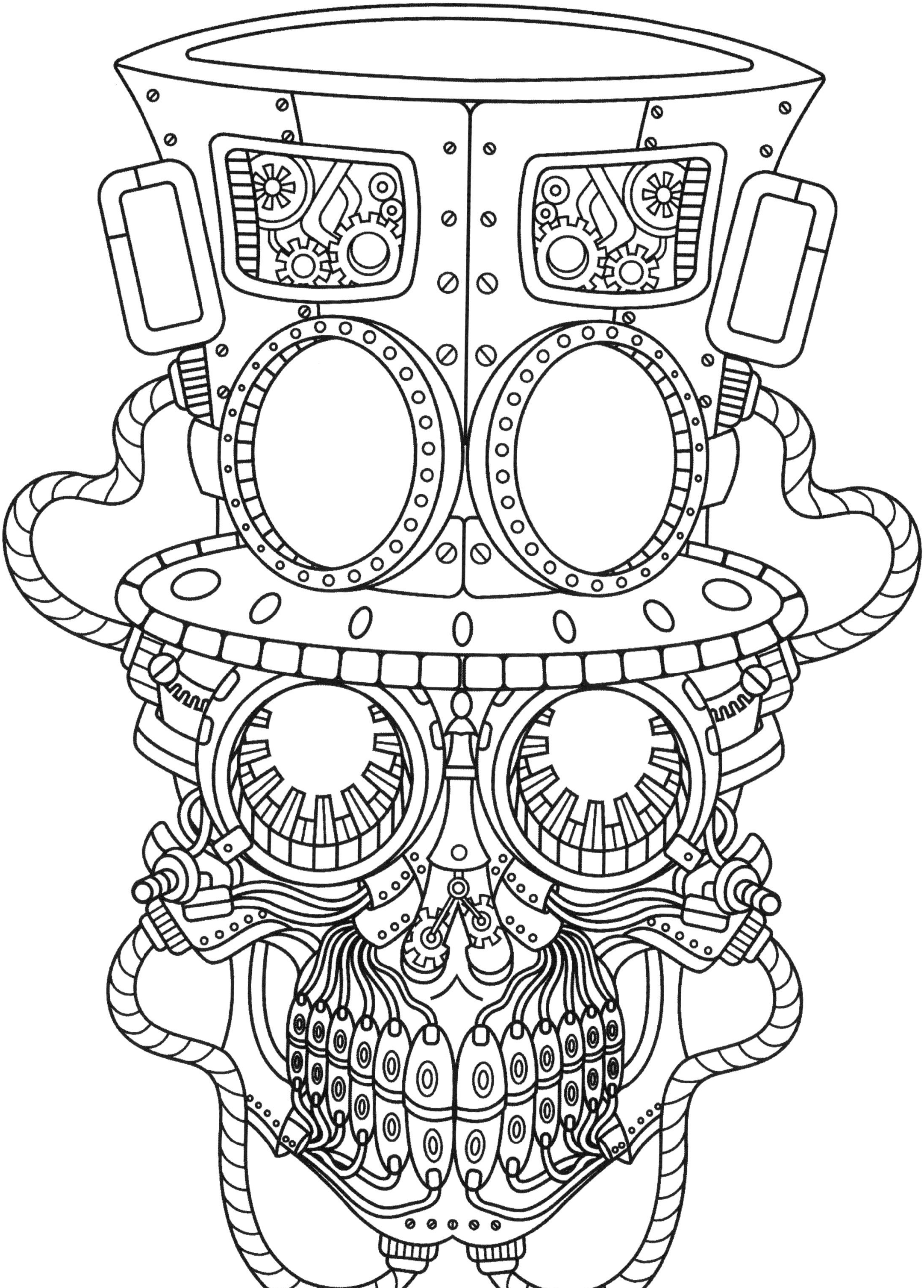

MEZZO ZENTANGLE DESIGNS

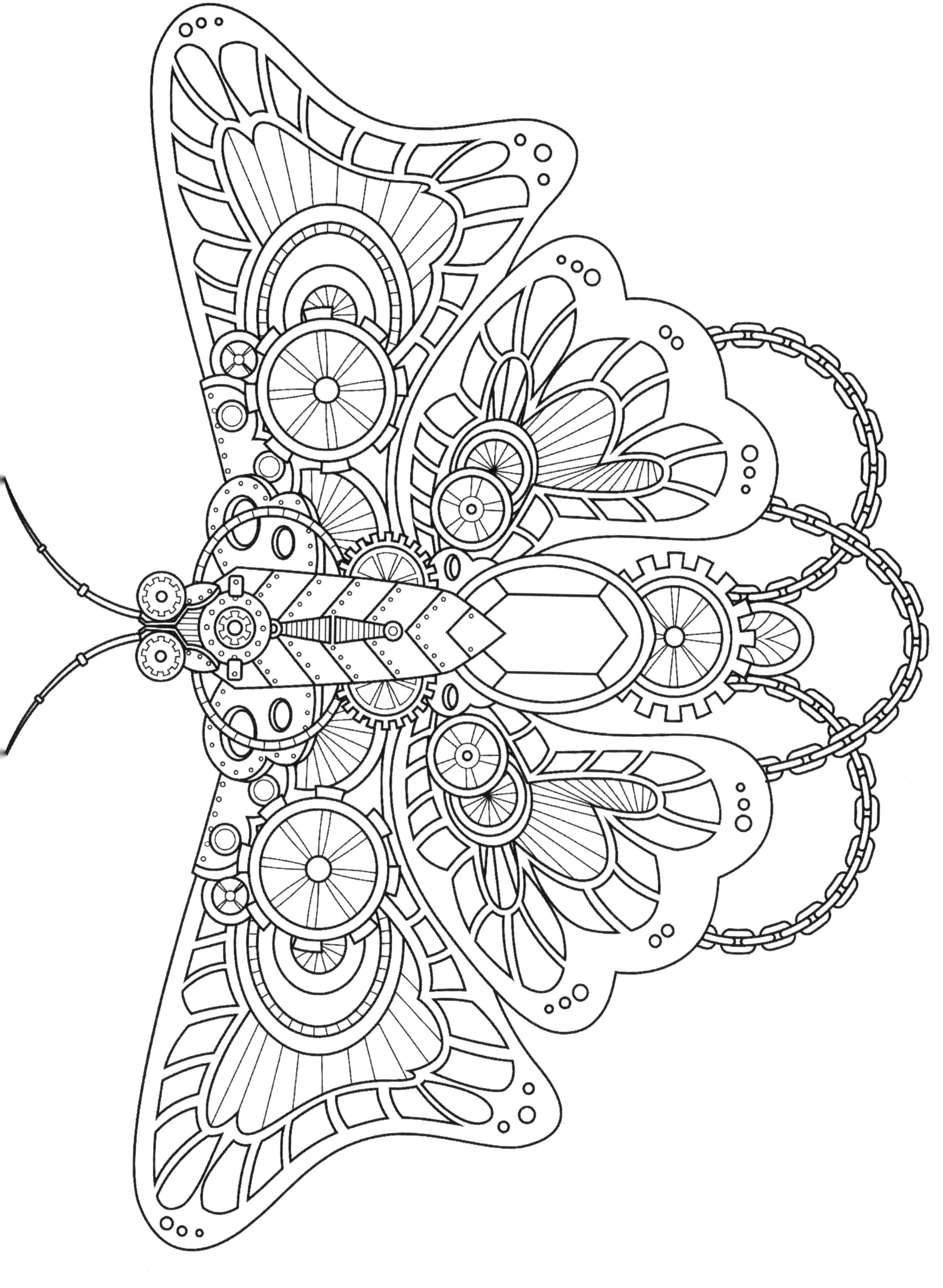

MEZZO
ZENTANGLE
DESIGNS

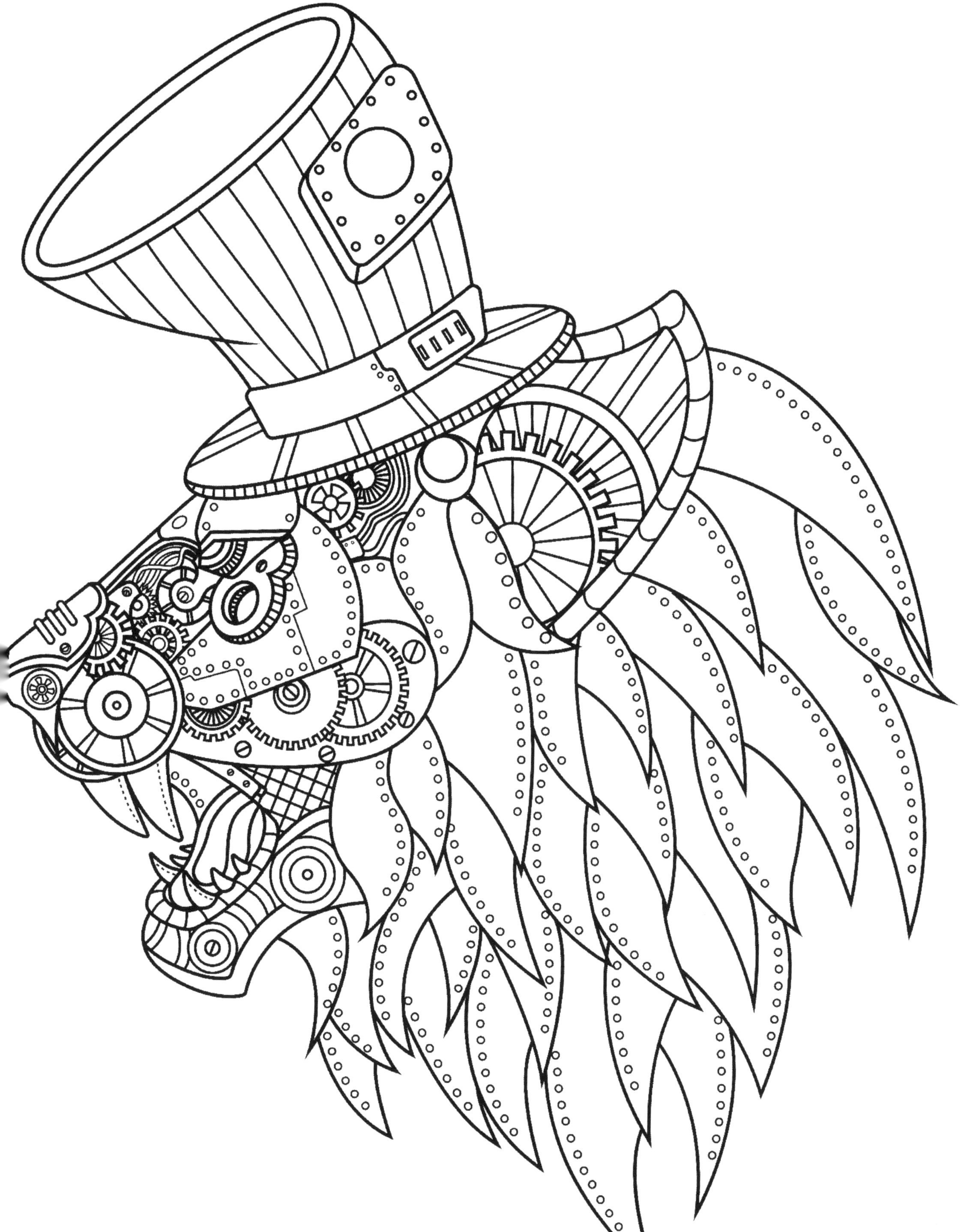

MEZZO
ZENTANGLE
DESIGNS

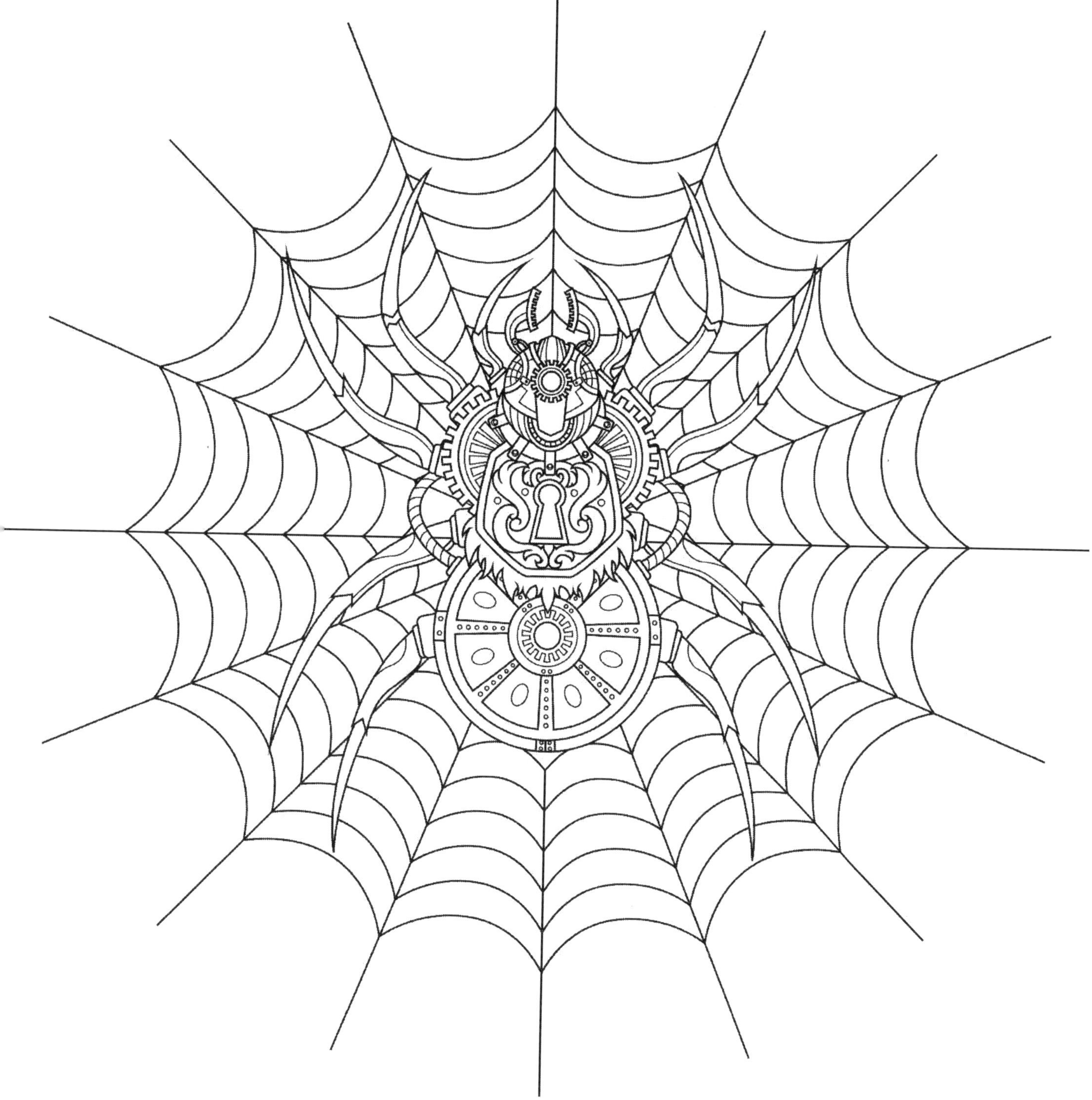

MEZZO
ZENTANGLE
DESIGNS

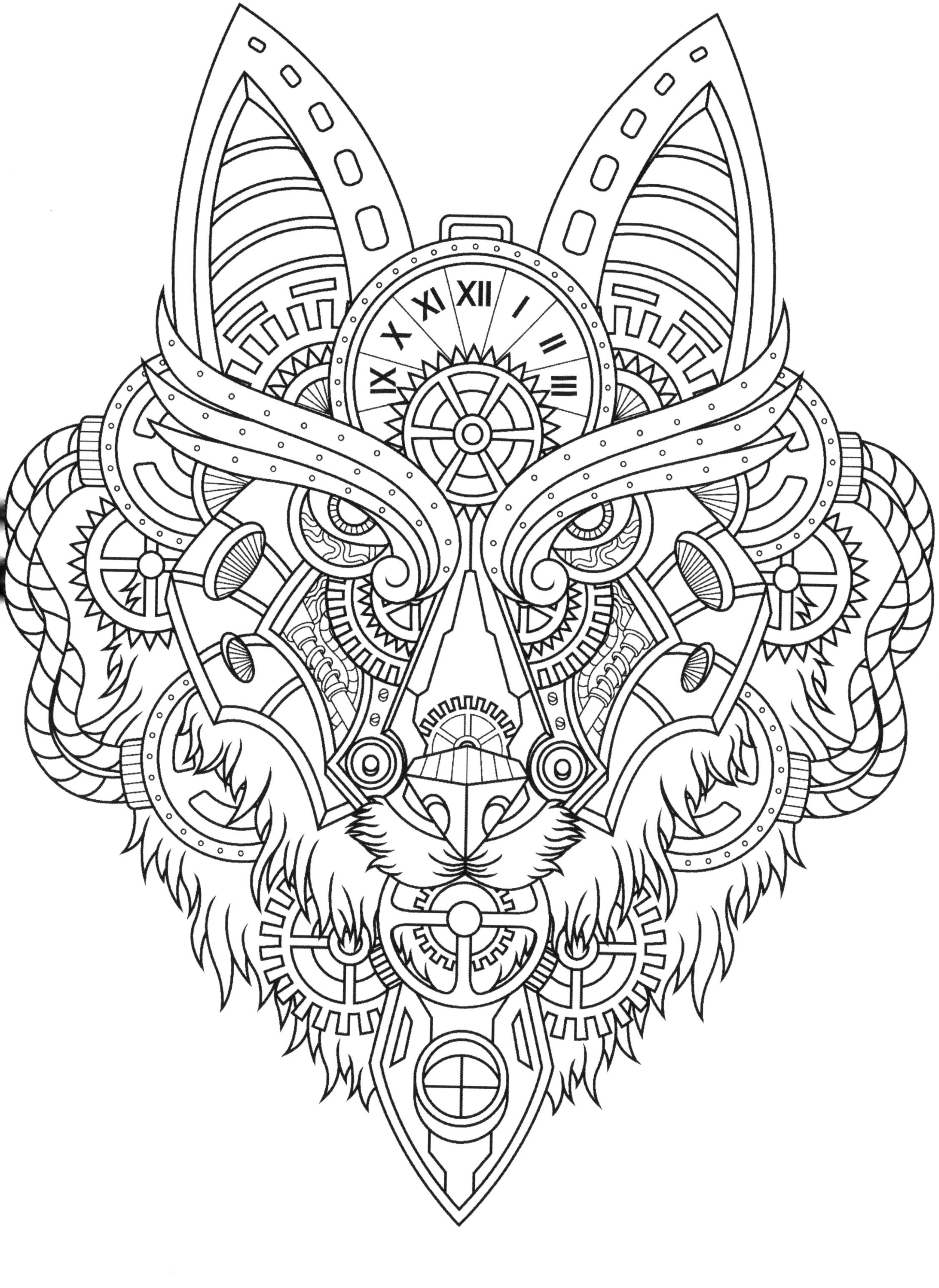
XI
XII
I
X
II
IX
III

MEZZO
ZENTANGLE
DESIGNS

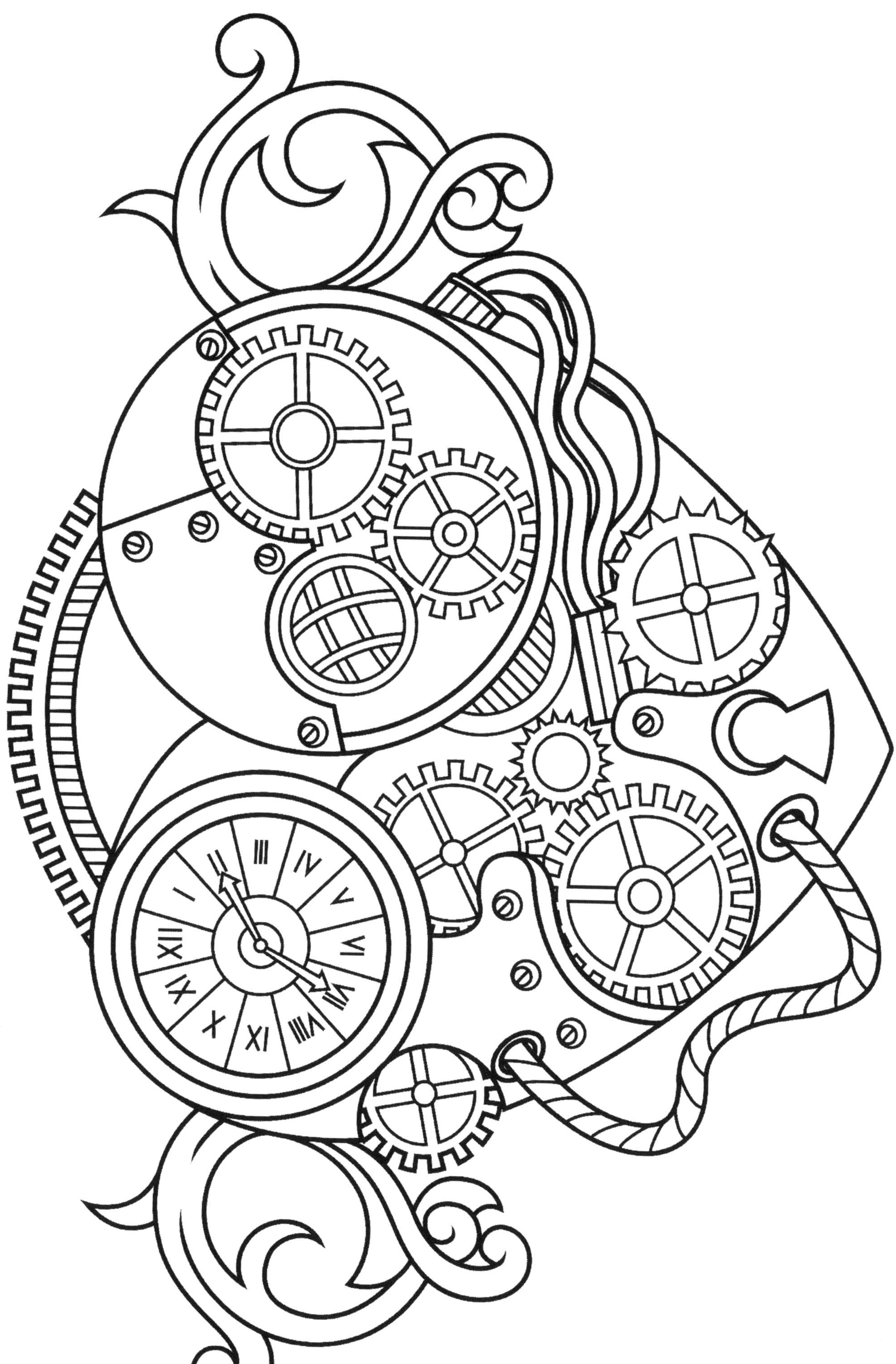

MEZZO
ZENTANGLE
DESIGNS

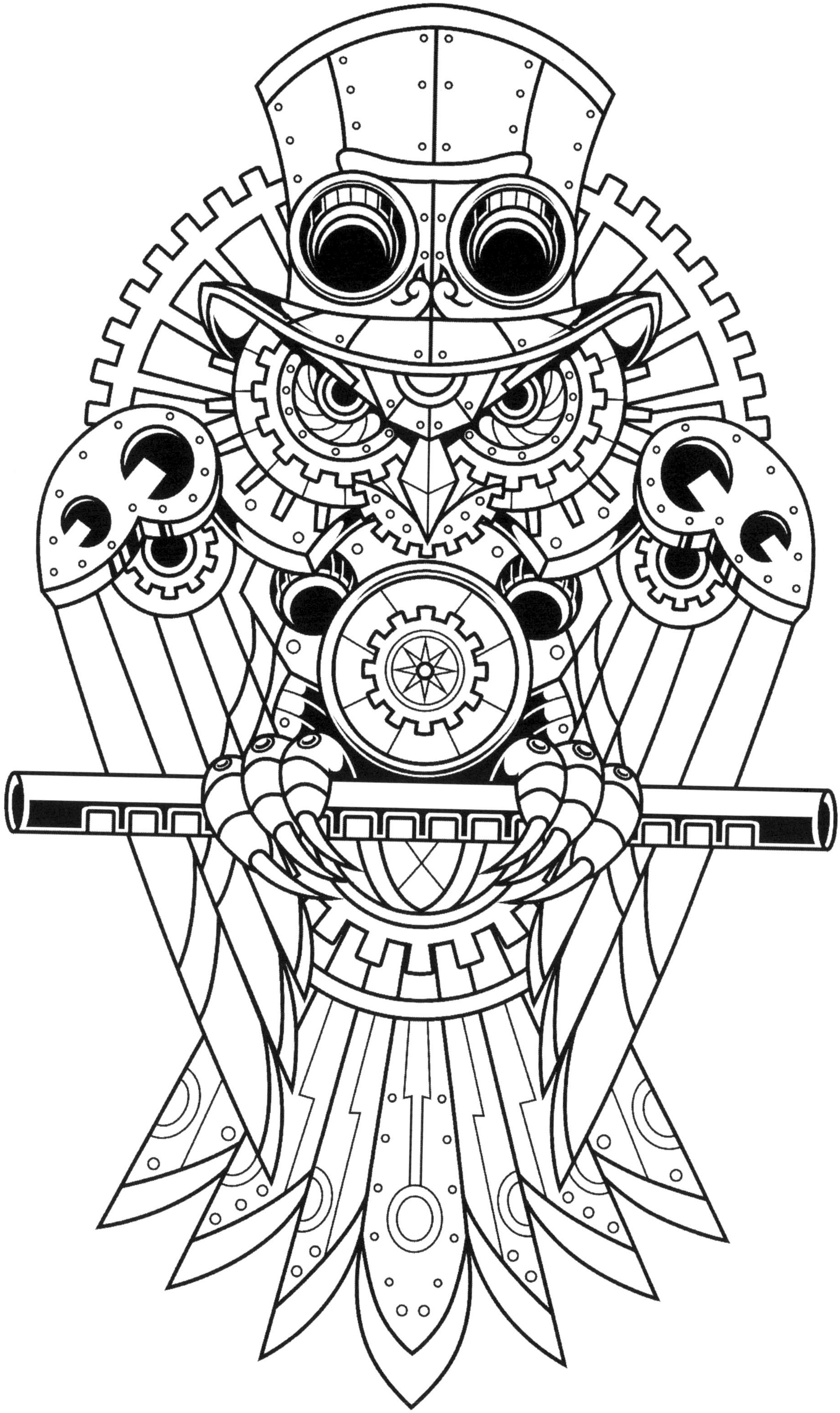

MEZZO
ZENTANGLE
DESIGNS

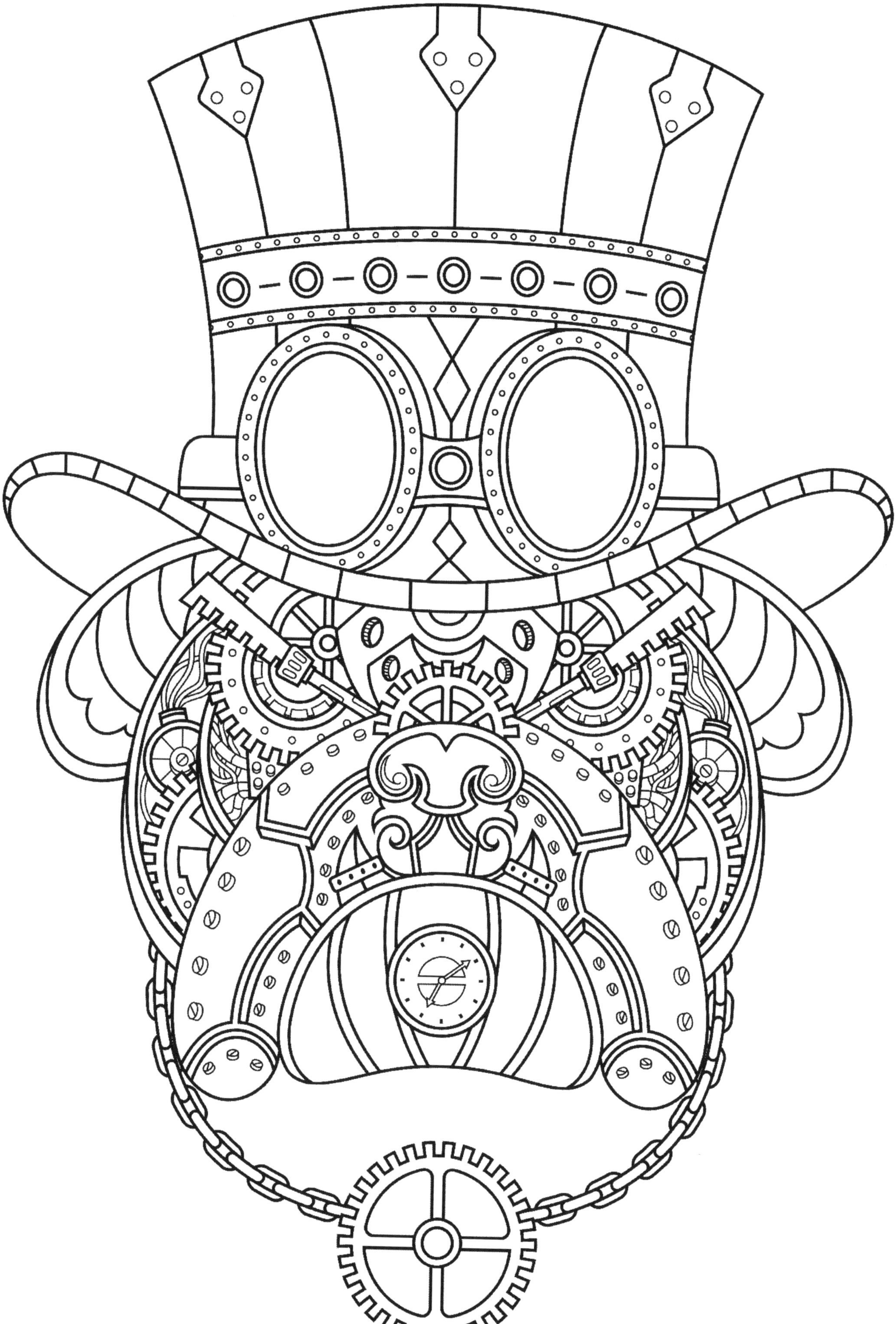

MEZZO
ZENTANGLE
DESIGNS

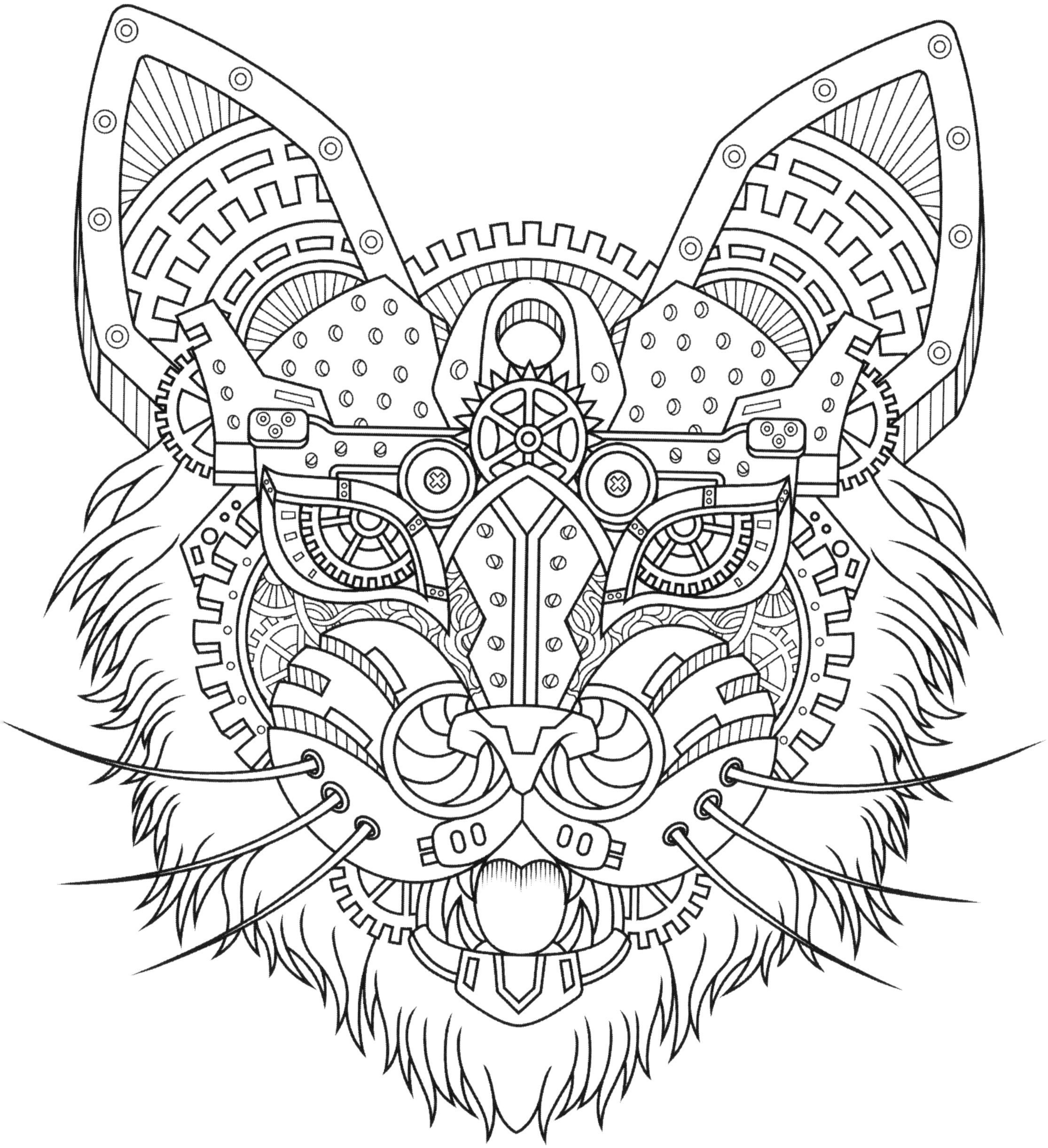

MEZZO
ZENTANGLE
DESIGNS

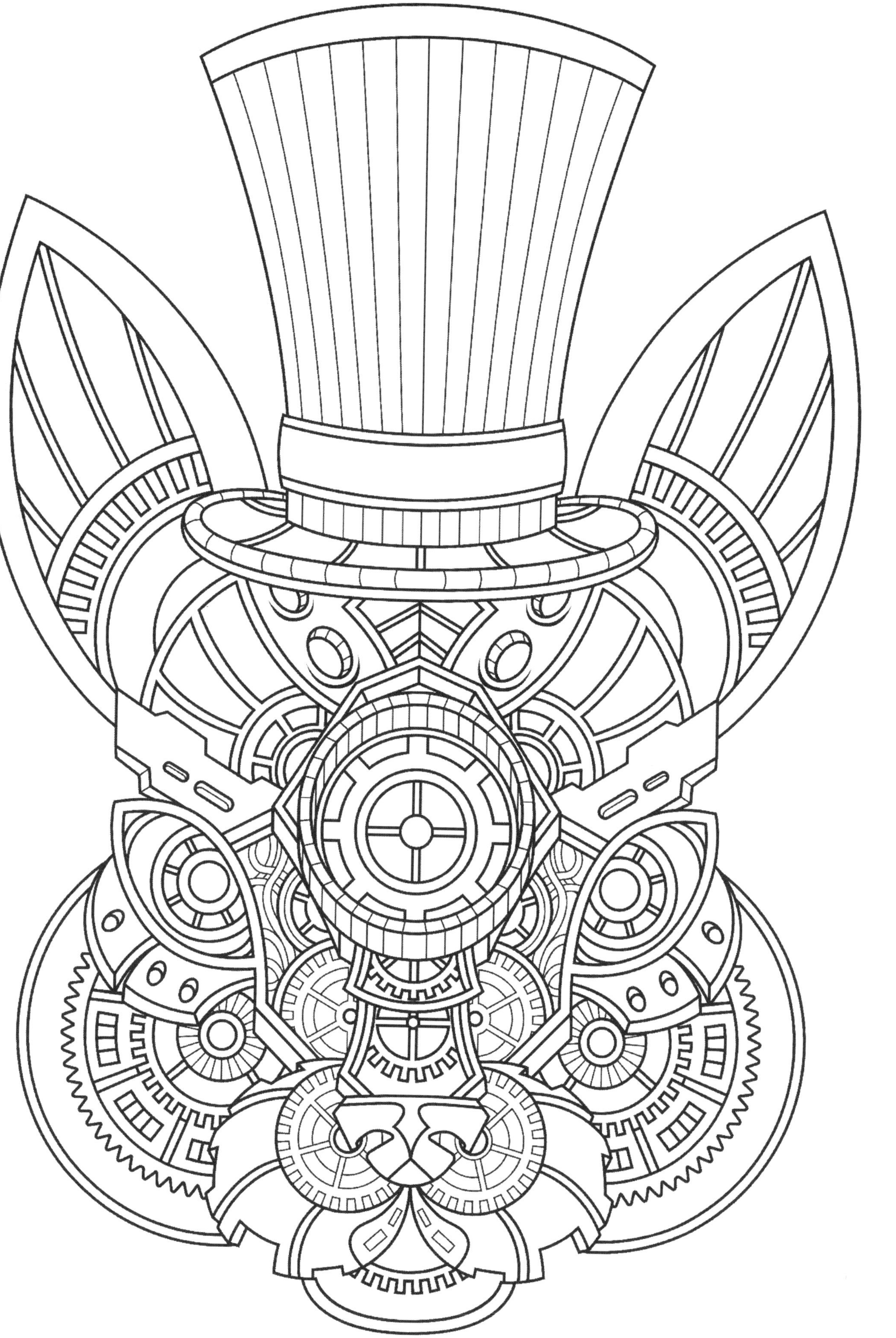

MEZZO
ZENTANGLE
DESIGNS

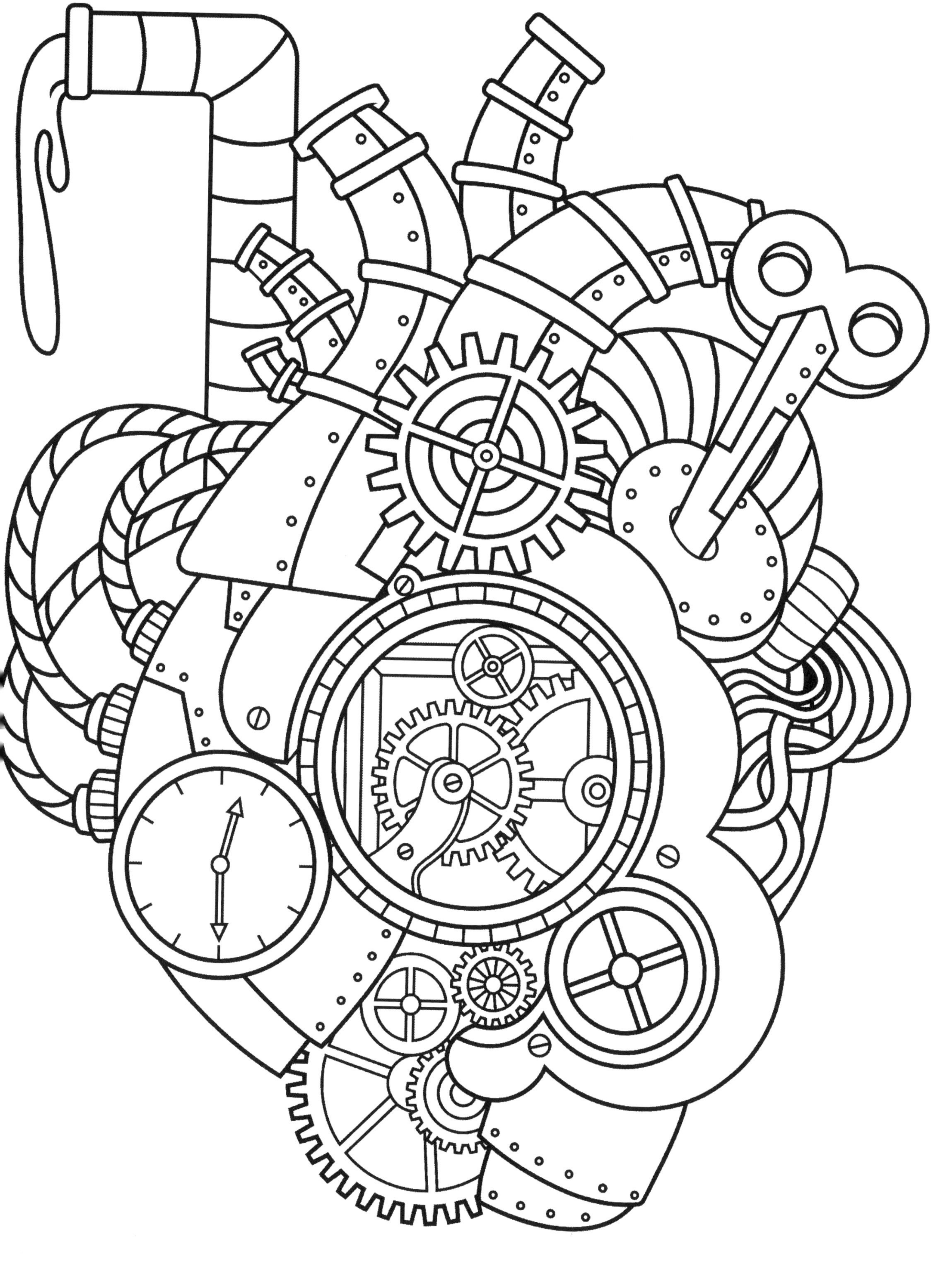

MEZZO
ZENTANGLE
DESIGNS

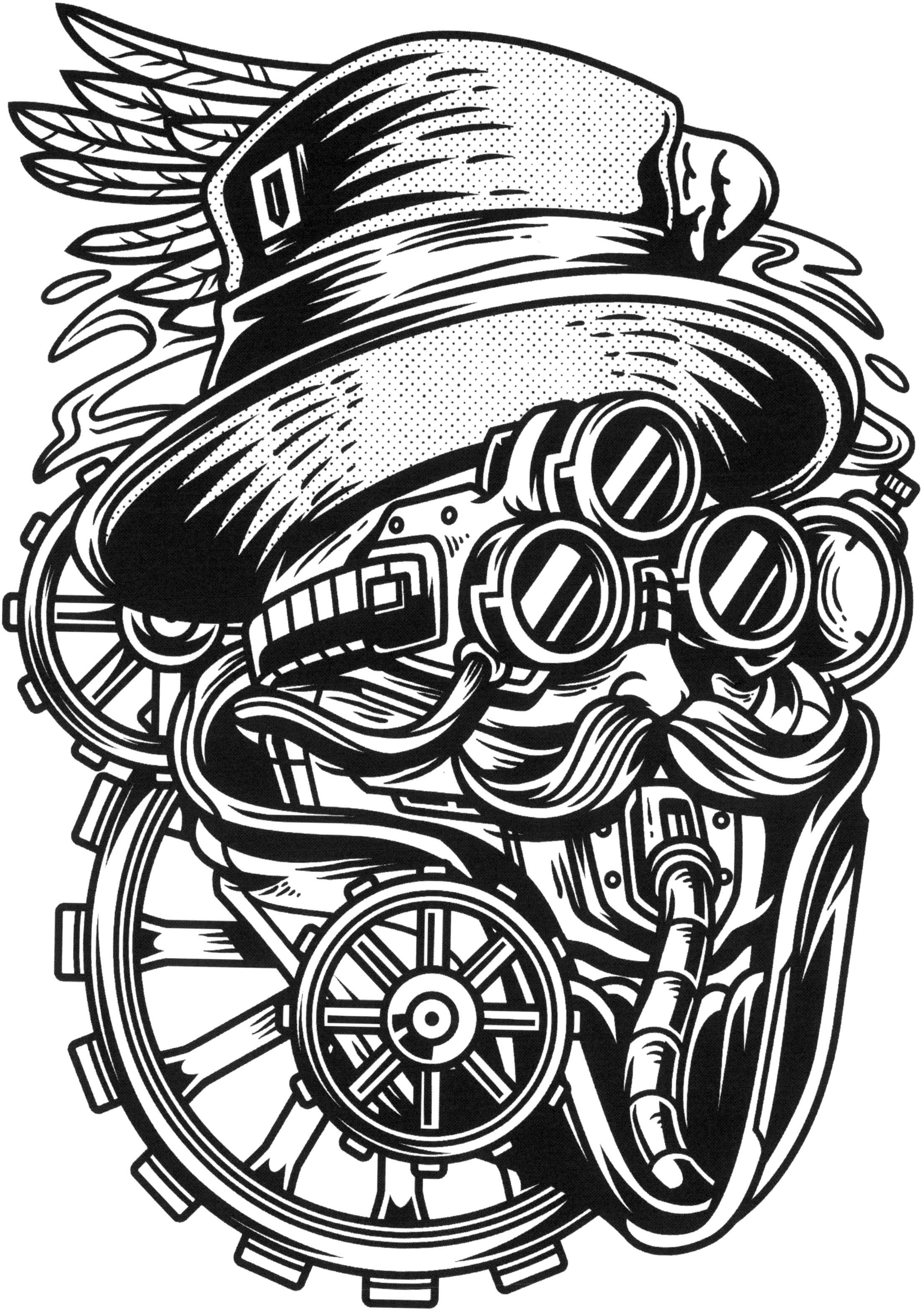

MEZZO
ZENTANGLE
DESIGNS

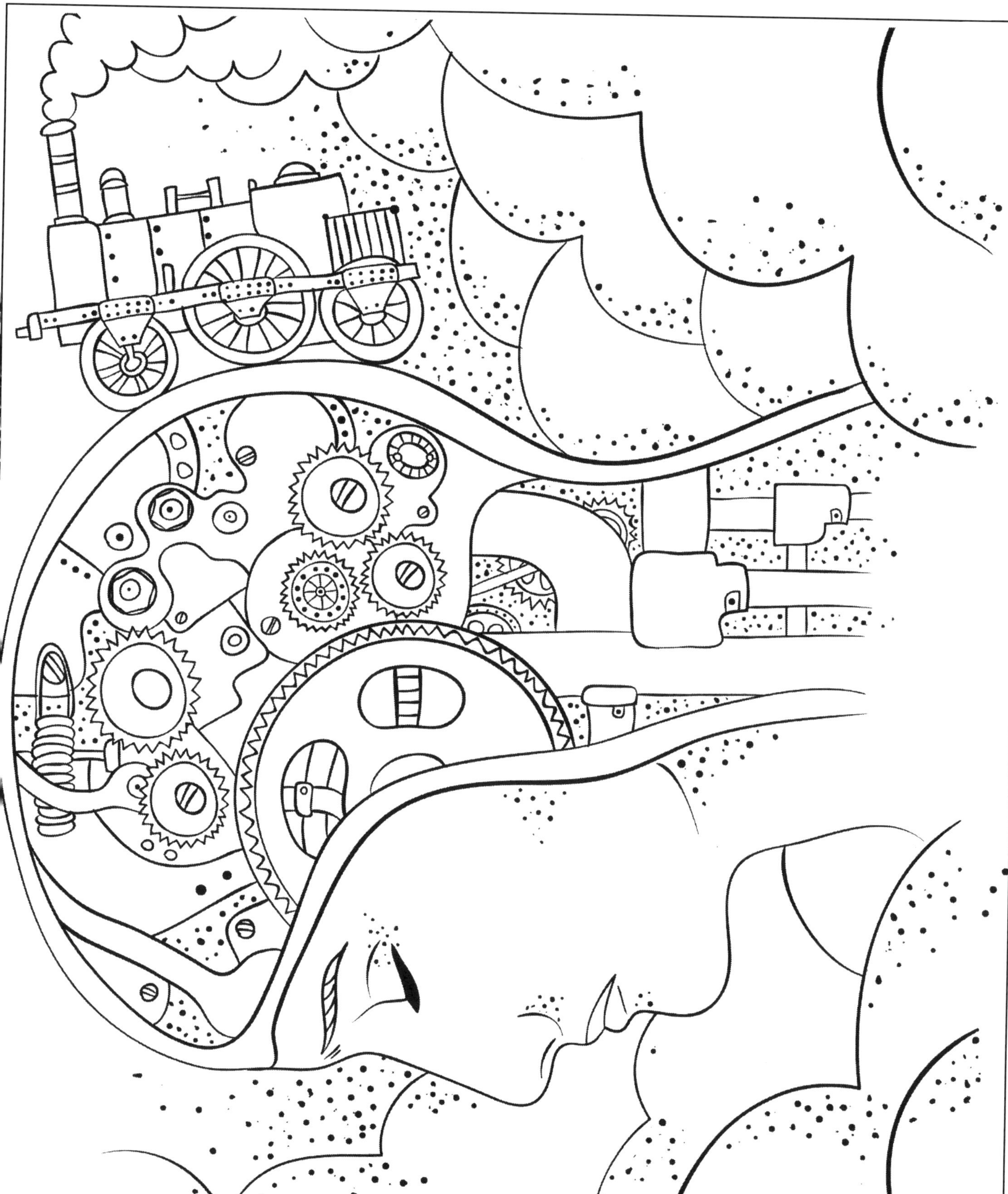

MEZZO
ZENTANGLE
DESIGNS

Made in the USA
Columbia, SC
15 August 2022